SPANK THE BOJOG EATING PUDDING ON A TRAMPOLINE

To prevent the world going to ashes

Konstantinos Mandilaras

Copyright © 2020 Konstantinos Mandilaras

All rights reserved

The characters and events portrayed in this book are fictitious. Any similarity to real persons, living or dead, is coincidental and not intended by the author.

No part of this book may be reproduced, or stored in a retrieval system, or transmitted in any form or by any means, electronic, mechanical, photocopying, recording, or otherwise, without express written permission of the publisher.

Cover design by: Theodora Kyriakou
Edited by George Demet & Heidi Goodall

Library of Congress Control Number: 2018675309
Printed in the United States of America

Contents

Chapter 1: Dodging emotions
Chapter 2: Property ladder
Chapter 3: Life is what we make it
Chapter 4: A sight of labor spots the slavery
Chapter 5: Educated social circle
Chapter 6: A day at work
Chapter 7: Convenience versus privacy
Chapter 8: Charitable organizations
Chapter 9: Top talent immigration
Chapter 10: Simulating normality
Chapter 11: What am I turning to?
Chapter 12: A chance in a lifetime
Chapter 13: Use of immense power wisely
Chapter 14: Make an entrance
Chapter 15: Guided Human Evolution
Chapter 16: Systemic downturn
Chapter 17: The world party of political parties
Chapter 18: Democratic backsliding
Chapter 19: Existential materialism
Chapter 20: Servants of technological advancements
Chapter 21: Inhuman rights in defiance of human rights
Chapter 22: Mediocratic media
Chapter 23: Nature's last call
Chapter 24: Accountability of the sheep
Chapter 25: A fair opportunity in a utopic collective
Chapter 26: Take it or leave it
Chapter 27: A dream comes true

To the mortal mankind fellow feeling

AUTHOR'S NOTE

When was the last time, a question took you more than one month to formulate, at least three months to research and over half a year to answer?

If you don't remember, my mindset could get you started!

How the heck, spanking a bojog (wicked monkey from Indonesia), eating something sweet (pudding) on a trampoline (used for exercise and fun), could end up turning our world into ashes?

SYNOPSIS

We are all contributors to the replacement of our literal life into an unpragmatic lifestyle.
In the early years of the 21st century, there is no return from that fact. The least we can do, individually as well as collectively, would be to simply attempt probing that actuality.

The main character of the book taps into his everyday aspects of life. Unexpectedly he gets the opportunity to do something, most of us would never have a single legitimate chance to experience, just sit back and see our life taking place.
At this lapse of time, he is able to recollect, but also evaluate his experiences. In a twinkling he realizes, that he has an unprecedented chance changing everything for himself but also the whole world. After a moment of hesitation, he decides to take the simplest action anyone could, talk openly and out loud to the core of chaos.

CHAPTER 1: DODGING EMOTIONS

During the last few days my brain had been on fire, overwhelmed by my life and old experiences, while I was unable to tame my thoughts, a swirl of darting images and transitions to different locations were leading me to unimaginable places.
How was it possible to see myself inside a very big room with several world leaders, all looking at me with some degree of despair?
I walked slowly left and right in the room and looked at them, one after another, feeling pretty relaxed. Something is very fishy here.

"Cornelius, are you still sleeping?"
"Sweet girl, no I am awake, thanks to you my love, thank you."
"Oh, baby boy, I am asking because you looked like you are sleeping with your eyes open. You really make me laugh sometimes, what happened to you, you look like you have aged about five years overnight."
"Ah! my sweet girl, better if I don't tell you, it's just another dodgy dream."
"Ha-ha, I suppose so."

It is finally Sunday morning and a headache after sleeping a bit longer than usual is testing me. Every time I open my eyes, I look at the clock next to the bed, more than once, to make sure that I am not late for work. Sunday is no different at all, I always feel like I overslept.

This was my wife talking. I love her to bits and yes, she knows me better than anyone. We have been together since 2010, got married last year in the local town hall in a very small, private gathering for a few people. Since then she has been keen to have kids, but I have held her back, for various reasons. Huge topic and I try to avoid bring it up with her.

"Baby boy, I feel horny today and we have no plans whatsoever."

As if I am going to avoid this Sunday motivation to have kids. I am not sure if everyone feels the same. After you get married, every time you make love, you think that this might be the first or another kid and somehow that puts you off the reason behind making love with your partner.

"Sweet girl, we have lots of plans today, you forgot?"
"Baby boy, I have only one plan."
"Well, hold your horses baby girl, we said we would get up as early as possible, have a king's breakfast, then get dressed and go for a walk in the park, to try taking this path further on behind the fence, remember?"
"Ouch, this, I will say is the lamest excuse you have ever given to avoid making love to me."
"No sweet love, we really said that three days ago. And

then we said we would go for a walk to the shops to the one-pound store and buy some of that dish washing liquid, that we keep forgetting and should get after all this time. We also said to sit on the laptop to search for the new pillows, we wanted to buy for the bed."
"Right, well, next weekend we have no plans, right?"
"Yes, sweet girl, we don't have any plans."
"We will spend all day in bed, making love, period."
"Ok sweet love, deal, next week this bed will need repairs."
"Hurray, I booked you for good now and I have proof! Look at this and listen to it."

After a few dreadful seconds...

"Oh! You didn't."
"Yes, I did."
No, you didn't, this is extortion."
"No, it is not, it's the recording the judge will hear at the court, at our divorce hearing, if we don't make love next week."

Gosh, she got me for good this time. She actually recorded me saying we will make love next weekend. I saved this weekend. I will think of something until next weekend. After all I know the pin of her phone!

Phew that was a close one. It looks like I am trying to avoid her, but it is far from it. As opposed to that, I love her dearly and in bed she is stunning. It is just we have various other pressing issues that really make me prioritize other things rather than consuming energy on anything else. You might think I am quite preoccupied and a shortsighted person, but I am not, as much as it sounds.

The considerations to take into account need to begin from way back before the time of conception and the subsequent aftermath. Just take a moment to think. What are we eating, what are our bodies growing on, what do we breathe, what are the environmental stimulations that we are constantly experiencing in most developed countries of the world?

Are all of those storing up in our bodies, sperm and eggs, to host and create, to begin with, a healthy kid?

If I put into the equation, the mental stress that all of us go through daily, then it becomes an impossible puzzle to solve and all of these have something to do with our individual DNA. I know, if everyone were thinking like that, our species would go extinct in a couple of centuries, since no one will want to have kids anymore. That is the other extreme and of course not the solution.

What is the solution though?

Not many people seem to care either way, since hundreds of kids are born every minute on our planet.

So, what happens to those hundreds of babies per minute?

People in developed countries have kids in moderation these days and at a later age, whereas in undeveloped countries they have kids like rabbits do, in 10s. This creates serious questions, but there might be some indirect explanation that keeps bugging my conscious mind. Many will say that in undeveloped countries prevention, education and a system that at least in moderation controls birth is non-existent.

However, have you ever also thought that in an undeveloped country you don't send your kid into a school to be molded into a state approved homogenous drone that never allows them to think outside of the prescribed consensus?

More importantly, in these undeveloped countries, you do not teach your kids to repeat information instead of how to think for themselves, so that they don't become a threat to the status quo! In an undeveloped country most likely your kid will not graduate from a university, that then will lead getting a job to pay the taxes and bills, in order to perpetuate the corporate system of indentured servitude for your political overloads. Maybe, all of the above is in the subconscious of many people living in the so-called developed countries and puts on hold bringing a child into such a society for such a life, except the ones that are simply selfish or rich. It could also be our primal instinct for procreation, or simply our desire to have kids in order that we live the patriarchal family experience during our lifetime. Some would also think, having kids growing up so they have someone to take care of them, when they grow old and are unable to do basic things anymore. Is it though?

It's a thin philosophizing line, and considering all matters I mentioned above, many of the current parents are determined to fight for a better life for their children and this fact in no way makes them selfish. But what if it makes them naïve?

You decide, and for a change make a decision without being politically correct and who knows you might surprise your own self. In the meantime, live the dream as long as it lasts, because the reality is so far away, that no human made telescope can even see it.

CHAPTER 2: PROPERTY LADDER

Being a part of the labor engine of the capital city I live in, working daily in a usually unbalanced set up, surprisingly makes my life pretty simple. I like the usual stuff, good food, traveling, socializing, and spending time with friends and family. How many of the things I like, do I actually get the chance to do daily though, is another question with a very sad answer. I try to keep active, doing a bit of cycling and walking in the park almost weekly, if you call that active. I have high cholesterol and an iron overload condition. Which one of the two, if not both, will one day kill me? I don't know. I have been suffering for the past few months with a pain in my right knee and for the past 6 months I have been getting piles almost every week, creating anal itching that makes me so uncomfortable. I like meat, a contributory factor of my piles, and with high levels of bad cholesterol, but on the other hand a good level of protein content. Nearly 40-years-old and I notice so easily the change in my body now in comparison to my 30s. Aging has always been a bummer, but not much I can really do.

My wife is healthier than me, it appears, and that makes me try to be more careful, mainly because I would like to stay alive and spend more time with her for as many years as possible.

"Baby boy, are you still in the bedroom daydreaming? Come on now, get ready we have to go out for the shopping, remember what you said an hour ago?"

Gosh she is right, I pulled the 'have to go out for errands' line to avoid making love and almost forgot it already.

"Sweet baby girl, I will be ready within ten minutes," I shouted from the bedroom.

I got ready and went out to the local shops with my wife to buy the things we needed. At the shops I couldn't help but notice the local people. The majority of them look sad. I always question myself, is it my perception of people or do they really look miserable, tired and fed up?
After we came back from the shops, we went for a walk at the park just across the ad hoc road outside our small flat.
Something was bugging me and now was the chance to bring it up, just to see if she is still on the same page.

"Baby girl, for the past 3 years we have tried to save for a deposit to buy a house. We have two thirds saved of the total deposit required, which you know it's the minimum, for a 2-bedroom house further out in the outskirts of the city, since we both are fed up with the city environment."

"Yes, sweet pie that's the plan and we have discussed it several times, what on earth are your concerns now?"

"Well, I keep thinking, based on the current economic climate, the city's general living conditions and rules of our society, our plan can be easily translated into a hostage occupation."

"There he goes again with his theories! How many times do we have to discuss this, it's just a small flat that we will be able to repay before we reach pension age."

She replied with motivation and the fed-up face.

"No wait a second girly girl, we will buy a house with a loan, and work our guts all our life to repay it. It's not rocket science that modern slaves are not in metal chains anymore but in debt, considering that in several developed countries, a house is repossessed almost every hour, over hundreds declared insolvent every day and the average debt of an adult is around nearly double from an average annual salary. Knowing these key statistics, published by each developed country every year, how can I convince myself that this is the best way forward for our future?"

"No one can be sure for the future, baby boy, that is why it is called future, we don't know what will happen. We try our best to go forwards, step-by-step and hope for the best-case scenario. We have talked about all these many times."

"Yes, we have, but how can you disregard, that we are all so brainwashed by the current society, that we will keep working our guts out until we manage to buy a house. Then we have to work all of our life to repay it and if we get long term sick or lose our job, we most likely become one more of those statistical numbers and loose the house, if no insurance plans are in place."

"Hmm, no, we will make sure we have insurance for all unpredicted possibilities, there are so many packages out there to cover you for any kind of unexpected occurrence."

"Ok baby girl, in other words we will not only buy a house, we will put a price tag on our 'existence' in a similar way our employers do the day they hire us."

"Baby boy, I think I have had enough with your moaning today, can we change the subject now?"

"Sure, baby girl, but just let me say this."
"No, I have had enough I just said."
"Just a second baby girl, because I get even more concerned especially when I also know that in most, if not all, so called developed countries buying a house in many cases means that the state still keeps the ownership of the land the house is built on. Consequently, we will end up buying what is on top of the land, not the land. And even more interestingly many countries provide you with up to 100 years' 'lease' to keep the house and then you have to claim it again. To put it simply, if you die unrepentantly without having made already the necessary provisions to pass it on, there is a strong potential the state takes it back, regardless if you have family. I know sounds far-

fetched, but what if.

Baby girl, I watch those documentaries on various TV channels, about people that have had enough, for various reasons, and went back to nature, found a cheap piece of land that no government or corporation care about and made it their home. Living in nature more or less like our primitive ancestors did hundreds of years ago, of course in a more practical and efficient way. I wonder, are those human beings the outcasts of our society and we are the driving force of evolution or the other way around?"

That was officially the end of this conversation, since when I bring up the subject of remote living in the wilderness, she immediately gives me the 'shark look', a common indicator of, 'shut up, I don't want to hear it and change the subject, now or you sleep in the couch tonight.'

We walked for another half hour at the park and returned home.

CHAPTER 3: LIFE IS WHAT WE MAKE IT

Where are my manners, I kept going on and on without introducing myself and be sure, my name is not 'baby boy', as my wife Ursula calls me. My name is Cornelius Spinster and I live in the outskirts of East London, England, U.K. I am 39 years old, originally from one of the small islands of Kiribati in the middle of the Pacific Ocean. My parents are still there, but not for long. Some of those small islands would most likely be flooded with seawater and most likely won't exist anymore before the end of the 21st century. Both my parents worked many years in hospitality on the island. As I was growing up, I realized that this life was not for me, so I decided to move to London when I was 21, to study Chinese History at University. It took me less than a year to come to my first executive decision. Studying at the university wasn't for me and soon I dropped out of the university studies. I spent the following years working on and off as a waiter, but soon realized that this also was far from a career I wanted. Next, I got a job at a company that ships containers all around the world and I learnt the job well, the secrets of the trade as one might say. For the past 10 years I have been working for the same company, as an accounts assistant manager, having a stable income, allowing me to basically live relatively well, go on holiday once a year and save one fourth of my income towards a deposit for purchasing a house. At the end of each year, I get a bonus, which more or less comes out as taking a 13th monthly salary per year! Am I a happily paid worker, I better leave that to your interpretation! Am I happy with life in general?

Well, this is the million-dollar question for most of us. Beginning with the fundamentals, all the years I worked, I had to pay to go to work. As a result of this, I always had to pay to leave work and return home. In other words, if I wanted a job to make a living, I had to pay a transport fee to go to that job. Obviously, I had to pay to eat at work, so I could keep my strength up for until the end of each day at work. This is a hugely accepted concept, paying with your own money in order to go to work, so we make some of that money back! What an amazing deal that is!

And I continue recollecting, are we happy working from since we remember ourselves, in order to be able to live in the appropriate rhythm of modern society?

Personally, taking this question into consideration and excluding its branching areas, the answer is a bit sad to say the least. If I take into account that I have worked for the past 18 years like a donkey in various jobs, I should first ask where am I standing now? Hmm, let's see, with a salary that with cutting down on quality of life and in many cases the quality of health care, I have ended up saving crumbs each month. Crumbs of money that if anything goes wrong, I would need to use in order to bail myself and/or my family out of a health problem or a financial stuck up situation.

Well, then no I am not super happy after all.

I have wasted more than half my life working, paying taxes, paying for a pension that most likely will be dead before I am able to use. Even if I am still alive when I am 67 years old, new legislations could crop this pension to less than, a scenario played out several times throughout the world for many decades.

How depressed I feel when I begin thinking about those matters. Even if my wife keeps saying to ease up on that kind of thoughts, avoiding the issues relevant to our life, do not make them go away, on the contrary it allows them to 'incubate' and in most cases become worse.

A large number of our fellow human beings have been consistently responsible for the consecutive world economic crises, recorded since the first century from loans for Roman houses until today. How unfair is the fact that all of them became richer after every economic crisis! So, what does this make us, the rest of the planet's population that ends up poorer after every world economic crisis? May everyone judge for themselves.

I worked nonstop, since I remember myself, and never got a 6-figure salary. My work never harmed my employer or the greater good of humanity and I still never got the 6-figure salary. So, to my naïve brain it means that if your job involves exploitation without ethics, then yes you might get a 6-figure salary. And wait, there is more to it. My manager has never even passed outside a university, or seen what it looks like as a building, at least I have done one year. My manager is not from Kiribati of course, he comes from the capital city of a country placed in the top 10 of the planet's strongest economies! But I accept, I am nobody!

What about the medical support staff, teachers, police officers, fire fighters and brainstorming scientists?

None of them getting anything like a 6-figure salary and I hope I am not surprising anyone, when I say that most of them are getting paid less than me. My wife works as a teacher, in other words, in a never-ending government experiment called secondary school. She earns significantly less than me, while she works over double the hours, preparing the new generations of the country to take over! So based on this scale, I, who arrange shipping containers to go from one country to another, am supposedly doing a more important job and getting paid more than a police officer or a teacher. I know for a fact that a 14-year-old kid could do my job, even better than I do it, however I know that a 14-year-old cannot police our streets or respond to a burning house or teach math to a class full of 16 year old students. And I am not talking about the extreme outliers and teenage geniuses that do wonders, I am talking about the 14-year-old from next door. Still, in our society's structure of employment accountability, my job is worth more than all others mentioned, whereas the bank manager jobs responsible for all economic crisis in human history, are worth more than mine. Go figure that out and please let me know what you come up with, because I come up with only one outcome:

Blame the ancient Greeks, for the creation of the first weapon of mass destruction that for centuries has been used to mask human exploitation in the name of 'democracy'? They created it and they couldn't contain it, control it or even teach it to the rest of the civilization properly, so who is going to take the blame now, the 21st century politicians? Ha-ha...

CHAPTER 4: A SIGHT OF LABOR SPOTS THE SLAVERY

Based on the early 21st century figures from the international labor organization, from the 7 billion people living on planet Earth, less than 3 billion are in any kind of employment and of which I humbly predict half are in part time employment or contract employment, meaning that at any given time they could be out of employment!

So, are the remaining over 3 billion people just chilling?
Well, that is an interesting speculation and if you 'trust' the published statistics, search the topic for yourself. A rough estimation could be that many would be over 60 and under 18, fair enough!
What about the rest, are they unable to work or are they in unrecorded black-market labor?
Isn't that a major failure of our society, having more than two billion people between 18 and 60, chilling! Although I doubt many of those people would think like that. Who would want to work, considering that their life will go through their eyes to serve the higher banker's purpose! Working until you grow old, unable to serve the banker and depending on the current situation of the state you live at the time, you get a cheap funeral!

Just imagine how differently I would have answered this question, and most likely the several billion of people, if work were structured for the greater good, instead of the greater wealth for the few.

How different my perception of work coupled with my productivity would have been if, for example, I were working 6 months per year with triple the salary I make now. Utopia hey! Well, no!

Just take a second and think, if the 'elite' of our planet have managed to reach outer space, tap in the core substances of the creation of our universe, as well as intervening at the molecular level of the human body, to say the least, I refuse to believe that they are unable to structure a prosperous society for all, where salary, work and lifetime of every human is celebrated equally, during their only chance of a literally very short lifetime.

So, after the long answer, once more the short one is no, I am not happy with my work. If anyone say they are, those are the systemic citizens feeding a system made for sucking our blood out of our veins for centuries. Fellow human beings blindfolded from a fake utopia with an expiry date, that is way shorter than you think.

It will be interesting to see what will happen when the current population rises to 10 billion in no more than a few more decades, where more food will be needed, as well as more jobs and water. Biofuels will take more and more of several types of crops, so I wouldn't be surprised, if the governments make us all farmers in order to cover food and fuel demands for the additional billion people. And when it comes to water shortages that would be the real puzzle. One in five individuals does not have clean water to drink, today in the early 21st century. I can only imagine how this will escalate. What we take for granted today, in the very near future will be rare and considered luxury. And as for the jobs, I do not need to be a genius to predict that more than 50% of the jobs done by humans today, will be replaced by mass-produced robotic workers. The word unemployed will cease to exist and the 'elite' of our planet will once more find a way to use humans in an alternative way.

CHAPTER 5: EDUCATED SOCIAL CIRCLE

It is already Sunday night and I am about to go to see three of my close friends, all Greeks! I know them from one of the restaurants I was working in. They were frequent customers and with time we became friends, especially when I quit the job. It figures! We meet to watch football matches and grill meat on the barbeque.
Although they are good guys and good friends, they all have called me a communist, anarchist and even racist. I would say I am a bit of everything. I am racist to uncontrollable power, I am communist to pretentious democracies and I am an anarchist to governments that abuse their power, especially against the poor. By contemplating my life in such a way makes me look like a bit of a prick, especially when I keep considering that the Greek creators of the so-called democracy are responsible for all this mess around the world today.

My friends though, reside on the other side of the life tables. They are all deep into the pretentious capitalistic bubble that make us all believe we hold a piece of that wealth. They are happy knowing that they are part of the sad fact, 99% of our planets' wealth is being owed by the 1% of the population and funnily enough they and I are in this 1%!

And there I am, just arrived at Kostas's house where we are meeting today. Manolis, George and Kostas are all there. I was planning to share my concerns with them, especially when during the last few days every thought in my mind feels like its ageing me by a year, but at the same time I want to banter with them a bit, so we don't get bored.

"Hello guys, I hope you had a good weekend with your better halves. I am so happy to see you all again. Can I just say something?"

They all start cheering, mocking me as always, knowing that I would go straight for it and stir them as much as I can, trying their tolerances on the hot subjects.

"Have any of you come up with a legitimate explanation for the fact, that every modern Greek out there keeps bragging about being the first country to have democracy, as opposed to trying to hide it as much as possible?"

I sent them into riots, they all began talking at the same time.

"Hold on a second, let me finish. Recorded history tells us clearly that Greeks could not only not control and expand the term democracy properly, but as opposed to that, they gave a way to all sorts of organizations and future governments, to use this so-called democracy to rip off the wealth of the planet at the expense of human life. And yes, they do it in the name of democracy even more nowadays."

George did not allow a second to pass and told me with intensity in his voice:

"Yes, it is our Greek ancestors' fault that when the humans on the rest of the planet were killing with sticks and eating each other, we were exercising democracy and human anatomy, get a grip Cornelius and spill your guts somewhere else!"

Well, there you go, that's why they call me all those names, my views are more than spicy and can begin a heated debate at any given gathering. All three of them considered as my closest friends are more educated than me. All three have their PhDs, however, none of them work on a job that is related to their academic knowledge and one of them will be repaying his university studying fees for most of his life.

And I continued…

"Let me ask you all something else. Are you happy with your decision to study at the highest level?
Just think of your current situation. You are all more or less within my age range, you have similar work experience and way more qualifications than I do and only one of you has a higher salary than I do. However, you all do work on disciplines that are way more important than shipping containers."

Hell broke loose in the room. It makes me laugh, every time you hear them complaining, but is it their fault?

Kostas came up first to defend their education:

"Doing my PhD was the best experience in my life to date. I have acquired knowledge that I would have in no other way. I have put my name next to great scientists, I have contributed to the scientific force to solve unanswered questions and at the same time I motivated and inspired many other students to carry on the work. I regret nothing."

Manolis and George nodded in an approving way, while Kostas added:

"My PhD gave me skills that I have used and can use for any kind of employment in the future. No other project could expose you to such a variety of complex daily tasks that have to all be completed by you. In a PhD research project, you are doing all the labor, all the marketing, in many cases the funding sourcing, the directing and the wrap up of each stage of the project. It is extremely intense and a major achievement at the end."

I couldn't agree more and without having done a PhD, I couldn't associate with their perceptions. I had to ask them without any strings attached:

"These are all much appreciated and respectful points, but don't you think you are one more reject of a scientific society following a narrowed agenda? Have any of you or your fellow PhDs during or soon after their work finished, realized that all their efforts were in the crude reality, strictly directed by the usual invisible 'elite'?

Didn't you all feel that the discoveries you made, with legitimate potential to aid the greater good, were in the end somewhat insignificant for the institution you worked for?

And you know, don't answer any of these questions I put forward. Just ask yourselves, if deep inside you felt that you are a great scientist, making those amazing connections at the Micro, Nano and Pico level, but at the same time you felt unappreciated after dedicating a large part of your life for the greater good."

This did sound a bit harsh, but none of them had anything to say, so I kept going:

"If the 'elite' are not about to make more money or gain more control out of your research, you are out one way or another. As for the people doing their masters and bachelors, they will first lose out on top jobs to the PhD holders that academia does not need and then to the ones that have never walked into a university but worked and gained experience on the job. The result is more than obvious, a society full of science graduates working as administrators or waiters. And let's look in this room only, between the 4 of us, there are 3 PhD holders in Biology, Engineering and Mathematics of which 2 of you work in a semi technical job. I admit that you get something back from the higher education, but the reality is too apparent to be missed. Universities are a selective moneymaking industry, far from aiming to aid the greater good.

Manolis who hadn't spoken since we had started talking, replied with attitude:

"Cornelius, based on your beliefs and your idea that everything we face as a society in the 21st century is the fault of Greeks due to them inventing democracy and us all losing the plot thereafter, then when it comes to the corruption in today's universities, we should blame the Arab woman that in 859 AD founded the first university to award a degree."

Everyone laughed, but I could not help it and went on:

"Manolis, when it comes to the Greeks, we will never agree and you know it, so we will pick it up again another time soon. As for that far too forward for her time Arab woman over a thousand years ago, I don't think that she would ever have had in mind our current evolved type of university, where money can buy you a degree, even a PhD, and I am sure this is not news to you. I am sure that she never visualised universities that get you in debt before you even make a start on your life. Universities run by out-dated managers', servants of the 'elite' caring primarily for their deep pockets. Taking a step back, you might want to ask me, am I being unfair to the ones that are still in universities, studying or working?
I can openly say, not at all, and the reason is because if I had the chance, I would do exactly the same. If I were doing a PhD and my research was welcomed by

the 'elite', I would have been another happy clone in secured employment. That simply makes me human, doing everything to survive in a society in which dinosaurs have been replaced with corporations and 'virus pandemics' with economic crisis and constrains."

All 3 of my friends started shouting, and George had to say his bit again:

"Why do you moan about everything and especially the ancient Greeks, like an old brat then?"

And laughed out loud, at least they weren't getting offended by any of my comments on their life efforts. I had to put it to sleep, it was getting late...

"I don't moan much, but as opposed to that, I am saddened. The reason is that those university researchers, including all 3 of you, have a title that by definition allows you to philosophize, whereas I don't. The difference though is that those so-called philosophers exercise their practice under a constant mind occupation, whereas I don't and what this might mean, it's down to individual interpretation."

We kept going on and on like that and the night came to an end soon after. We all had to cut it short, because we were working the next morning. It takes me about half an hour to drive home from Kostas's house, in my 17-year-old car, that is more or less a death trap driving it, but not a chance I can afford anything else at the moment.

On my way home I could not stop thinking about the leftovers of the conversation I had with my friends, in particular for all the masters and bachelors graduates and their parents believing their kids were getting some valuable tools to cope with the requirements of our evolving society. How sad it keeps making me, the fact education is not free and cutting-edge research is narrowed to the minimum. Wouldn't it be better, when we are about to make a decision for our next steps, to take a break and reflect for as long as possible, before we do what the 'scenario' says?
Or would that make us lose on the momentum time frame thus to the competition. Well, yes, we would most likely lose big time, knowing especially that the current societal system has made sure to rely on no single individual, no one is irreplaceable, the world will function as it does, after you, I or anyone else gets out of the everyday picture. Sad but true!

You see the brain of a human being is an abyss and it is currently the only place that none of the 'elite' or their branches have managed to enter in full. We could still think, dream, wonder and even philosophize, therefore most likely for the next few years it is the only part that remains for us common humans to have ownership. But we have to use it mainly by blocking inputs that block its fundamental function, which is constant development. I am terrified of the inventible fact that this alleged brain freedom won't last for long, since technology does its best to prevent it from so many directions.

Finally, at home safe. My wife is already in bed, asleep, so I have to be quiet, take off my clothes and go to bed like a thief. I will do my best to put a stop to the blazing thoughts in my brain, because I need some sleep, I have a big week ahead.

CHAPTER 6: A DAY AT WORK

It is Monday again, the day only a few people look forward to. Getting up and ready to go to work, using an overcrowded train that makes so much noise. At least if I manage to find a seat, I get the chance to read the fake news.
I get my news from the Internet, like the previous generations were getting it from the newspaper and television. I watch TV programs, but I have become too sensitive for mainstream television and the reason cannot be simpler, there is too much advertising and too much directed news that even the dog I don't have would have noticed by now. One of my extended circle friends, who is a psychologist told me recently that I exhibit signs of early psychosis, after I told her that it bugs me lot, when I read debates about capitalizing the word 'internet' in its written form. But it is not the word Internet really, it is what its being used for and how we common people have become life sentenced prisoners to it.
Take some of the technology giants of the early 21st century for example. Those are companies hungry for power and not innocent innovative establishments that work to improve the greater good of humanity.
Do they follow user movements, search habits, preferences of products and create psychological profiles in order to sell this information to the highest bid-

der?
Have we ever thought, that by now, those companies are not even controlled by their registered owners, but they are autonomous software programs that develop into something that we can only visualize in sci-fi movies?
Still think it is too farfetched to be true or not?

Hold that thought, because I am actually at work, I just got into my office and my manager is looking at me, telling me only with his eyes, 'you look a mess and its only Monday morning, first day back from a weekend.'
If only he knew what is going on in my mind. I sit a couple of hours at my office workstation, pressing the same buttons for authorizing shipments to go from one place to another and then grab one of my colleagues to go for a quick coffee break.

Ben is Chinese, born in London. A very nice guy, good worker and keen to grow within the company. He offered to take me out a couple of years ago. We went to an Asian buffet restaurant, eat as much as you can style. He insisted that he would pay that day. We both had eaten 5 full plates of all different types of food. The next thing I remembered was spending 2 days at home with food poisoning and spilling my guts out for good. I never told him. As we sit on the coffee couch area of the office, he takes out his phone to look at the social media applications. It felt like lightning stroke, seeing him crudely disregarding my existence just like that, so I asked him,

"Ben, if approximately half the population of Earth currently uses the service of Internet, a tool that after the military exploited it, then became available with the intention to improve our society, why has it become easier for all of us to receive news, which we have no way to ensure is valid news?"

No response whatsoever, but I continued regardless:

"At the same time while we distance from one another, if we want to send our news or views into the masses of users, we are either being blocked or would have to pay large amounts of money to do it and then get blocked. Who benefits from the Internet in reality?"

He raised his eyes, looked at me, smiled and continued looking at his phone. In other words, a pathetic zombie. He was immersed into the invisible social media world of his new supposedly smart phone. He is a lost cause and he is one of the many people out there strengthening my worry that we will never see a free mindful society again.

Human interaction has greatly declined over the past 20 years and it's only the beginning. We are bombarded by constant stimulants everywhere we look. Internet, advertisements, TV, radio with the majority of them trying to convince us of either to buy something or believe that their idea, product or group is better than all the others. The incredible aspect about it all is that we also have to pay for this information. We pay so that we get to see the options we have to choose, which product we will purchase, by again paying for it! Pay twice, for a product that we have no clue if it even does what we want it to do and most likely we don't actually need in reality.

We have been transformed into biological products with several examples, where humans are the product for sale. If you don't feel like a product every time you use a freebie, then job done on you, let's go on to the next individual who hasn't figured it out yet! Think, whenever you find something online or offline for free you go for it, trying it, use it and immediately you become the product, not the item you just tried out. The second you begin consuming it, testing it, using it, the company collects the crumbs of data you leave behind, either online or offline. But how can we not do this, when our life is so digitally interconnected, that once we cease using such facilities or offers, we could soon find ourselves outcast.

And like it is not enough being worked by the Internet, it gets even more chaotic when I come across terms like dark-net, black-net, crypto anarchy and so on. I wonder what some of the less than 2 billion online users' insights are about those alternative options.

Apparently, anyone visiting the darknet online areas with the appropriate amount of money, could buy the design for a handgun print. They can then hire or purchase a 3D printer that will then print that gun design for real.

So which criminal needs the gun traffickers or illegal drug dealers anymore? Darknet it is!

It makes me consider, who made the darknet and who do they expect to use its services?
Is it the police that wanted a platform to monitor and separate the normal dumb internet user from the smart threat to the system?
Is it the actual people that wanted to find another medium to traffic their illegal merchandise? Is it some corporations with who knows what motives?
Or is it some people who felt fed up from being tracked so much and wanted to create a platform that they can communicate without being monitored and eventually it has been used for illegal purposes as well?
As if I know, but it is as with everything else, when humans are the actual product, everything around us leading us on a one-way road, to be consumed.
Well, pointing the finger is too easy. Overcoming the convenient way to look at something out of the ordinary and thinking behind the short lines, is the real challenge.
Unfortunately, the monopoly of the World Wide Web consists no desire to protect our society, as opposed to that their target has always been and will be, to gather as many followers as possible by affecting the quality of news, education and consumption of goods. Freedom of mind is rapidly going extinct and sooner than many predict it, will be taught in history books as something primitive.

I am back in the office now and we have this large monitor on the wall, to play the live news from the different mainstream news channels all day long on mute, just subtitles.
I keep moaning about the fake news but sometimes I am stunned, when I see some journalists grilling their interviewees like a stake on fire.
Most of the time I question myself, do I believe them? Is it possible that a journalist would grill and in some cases indirectly insult prime ministers or CEOs for several minutes in front of potentially millions of viewers?
This fight in my brain is never ending, do I believe it or not?
It is after all, an admirable action if it is real, or worth an Oscar award if fake.

Watching the news from different worldwide news channels is an interesting exercise, if you speak the local language of course. Speaking a second, third and even a fourth language these days, is like you have won a mini lottery. But if you don't, then you rely on translations that are somewhat inconsistent.
Sometimes I ask myself, why care about stuff like that?
I remain silent and quickly change my thoughts!

With this and that, time to go back home now, after a not so much of a productive day at work. I spend most of the day fighting my own thoughts, knowing very well that I most likely will waste my time thinking all of it. The time has come to walk down the road towards the train station, fight my way on for a seat that at the end will not get. A trip that I pay very expensively for, in a train where I will be pushed, farted on, sneezed on, stepped on and even pushed out of the train, if I am anywhere near the door. But it is standard procedure, when you want to sell a cheap item expensively, put next to it something very expensive and say look how expensive this is, so it looks as if you are getting a bargain, whereas in reality you are thieving the person in front of their eyes. That is exactly what I feel when I see images and videos from transportation facilities in the capital cities of some countries, that they have employees pushing the people in the trains, stuffing them worse than they do the chickens on mass production slaughter farms. Of course, when I watch those places, I say that I am fine here, to be farted and sneezed on and pushed out of the train from time to time.

Not to mention travelling abroad. Taking an airplane to go anywhere, it takes, door to door, more than 5 hours from any country on the same continent. Just think of the wait to be picked up, traffic towards the airport, then a crowded airport, cue at check in, wait to board, possible unprecedented delays of flight departure, slow flight to save airplane fuel, landing delays due to air traffic, slow getting off the plane, long walk to customs, more cues, wait for luggage, wait to be picked up, traffic to the final destination and then you are there! Try not forgetting that in most of these steps, we are treated like potential criminals, whereas the real criminals are using private jets and get in and out of every airport from the back door!

I am back home and feel more tired from the commute, than the whole day at work. I will eat some salmon, fed full of carotene to keep the red color, looking good in my consumer's eye. I will then relax on the couch that I have been paying in installments for the past 2 years and will continue paying for the next 3 years, maybe then watch the news that a biased TV channel owner has chosen to show me and before I am to go to sleep. I will choose to watch a vampire series that will make me feel again better, since there are no vampires in real life that threaten our society, to my knowledge! I need to put my brain on hold tonight, so goodnight.

CHAPTER 7: CONVENIENCE VERSUS PRIVACY

It is Tuesday morning and I feel mentally broken. I called in sick, so no train, no Ben and until I manage to settle my mind, no working for others. I will try to focus on myself. I had my wife asking me all morning if I was alright, if I wanted any help, because she could see, something was bugging me a lot, especially calling in sick. If I were to say I feel that my worries involve world matters, most likely she was going to slap me and ask me for a divorce, before the coming weekend, so I reassured her that I had a bad stomach and left it at that.

It's 7:30am and I am already laying on the couch with the news on TV. They keep going on and on about this group, the 'anonymous'.
I am trying hard to find an action against humanity that this so-called anonymous group were involved in. On the news their name came up on a general report, after several governmental records were hacked throughout the world a few days ago from undetermined hacktivists. Anonymous, like maybe some other hacker groups can make a difference, based on what they have done till today.

They have the means to contribute to a major change

in the world, but why don't they?

This raises major questions to the poor mind of the common person.

Are they restricted from the chasing they get from the different governments? Are they the actual government, as it is common practice from most governments to create an event and use it afterwards to impose new control measures on the citizens?

Are they pretentious crooks that from every hack become richer, while they pretend, they are impacting the norm of the system on behalf of the common people?

At the end of the day, do they care what the public thinks of them?

I doubt it, but if one in a million, they are what we nobodies think they are, I really hope they go quiet for a bit of time, and plan something that would really change the modern slavery that humanity is undergoing nowadays. I don't believe the little disturbances of the norm they usually cause is enough, we have seen that more than once.

Maybe this could justify the fact there are people on the planet using the 'dark web', as the only medium of communication and exchange of 'goods'.

Many of those people live in countries with restricted freedom of speech. In these countries, if you go out and say I am gay or atheist, you might be prosecuted and thrown into prison. So sad. Here it becomes more interesting. People living in the 'free world' countries, can go out and say we are gay and atheists at the

same time and no one will even bother really. So how does this relate to free will, on the whole?
What if we live in places of the world that are called the 'free world', whereas in reality those places are the ones, which are free from real free will? Reflect on that and an aneurism could be your next step!

Our every move is monitored so much, that not only are we are used to it, but it also feels normal. So how can it be justified that the countries where free speech is not allowed, and access to communication is restricted, are the few remaining places mainly attacked by the leaders of the free world?
Maybe because quite a few of those countries are considered to be hubs for organizing world terrorism, based always on the view and intelligence gathered from our free world leaders. But what if terrorists are not that legit after all and are a product of the 'elite', to justify their actions towards removing all kinds of privacy from the 'not yet free world'?
And it makes it even more fake, when they make us believe that since most of us are not doing anything wrong, why care so much about our privacy and allowing all of our private data to be accessed. Our privacy is a pathetic battle, which we lost years ago, and no human rights organization could ever get it back. Convenience versus privacy is the price to pay. Not caring about privacy because we have nothing to hide, is like you are not concerned about freedom of speech because you have nothing to say. But is it our fault to think like that or have you been conditioned

over generations?

CHAPTER 8: CHARITABLE ORGANIZATIONS

Some are trying to help by forming other types of organizations, specifically to help humans and sometimes human free will!

Most come in the form of charities to help people with mental or other health problems, economical or war refugees, poor or homeless people, types of foreign aid and the list goes on. Either way, do they end up being successful and how could someone measure success?

No chance, for two reasons.

All of these organizations are made by humans, so immediately there is some bias within the concept, some underlying interest will be involved, while they help someone in need and that is enough to throw the aid out of its aims. The second and most obvious reason is that it becomes even more complicated, when in some cases governments get involved and no government will do something for nothing. There will always be something they want in return. So, we end up with services that the most vulnerable desperately need and the ones providing it have an agenda. Of course, there will be legitimate organizations that provide substantial aid, but what are the odds they are winning the battle of capitalism and most of all, will they be able to provide us with a measurable result in 50 years from now?

Let's say that at least those organizations are trying for the greater good, even if it's with an agenda. What about all those so-called organizations, underground clubs and societies that allegedly operate in the shadows?
Is it the most boring conspiracy theory existing or are they secretly running the world?
Although some novelists and journalists, have from time to time published names, locations and even actions with associated events that implicated these groups of people, the effect it had on most of society was simply zero. And I am asking, if those organizations were working for the greater good, why keep their meetings, participants and activities secret?
From one point of view, someone might think those groups of people are so influential and powerful that a report here and there from a small-time journalist craving a bit of attention, will not even scratch the surface of their agenda. But on the other hand, it might be possible that all of those reports, are a mere manifestation of a pure 'nothing' for us common people. And why could that be?
Well what better way, when the time comes to have screwed our planet and everything on it completely, to then put the blame for it all on 'the nothing'? Especially because I doubt any of us really question, why we allow ourselves to be brainwashed throughout our lifetime, to only really care about how well fed we are, our football clubs and sending dick pictures?

It feels like I only blinked once, and it is already evening time. My wife is due to come back from work soon and I should cook something, especially after being at home all day. I still have those unbearable headaches though and have had one throughout the whole day. I cannot explain why I want to hide those headaches from her. Maybe because I am sure it will pass sooner or later and want to avoid her worrying about me.

The rest of the evening passed in a more or less relaxed manner, after my wife was back, we ate while she was telling me how her day at work was. I told her that I was feeling a bit better, but I was planning to stay off work all the week just in case I had a bug that I might spread to the whole office. She insisted that I should go to the local general practitioner to be checked up, but I reassured her that I knew where the paracetamol was in cupboard if I needed it!

I was a bit anxious, as if I had to tell her what is going on really, but before I had the chance to finish my thought, she said that straight after work tomorrow, she would leave for a work trip for a week. That was it, the window of opportunity, first not to worry her with my dodgy situation and at the same time, use these extra few days to get to the bottom of it. That way, I would let her focus on her work without worrying about me as well. She soon kissed me goodnight, reminded me that the coming weekend making love had to be transferred to the following weekend and off she went to bed. I remained in the living room with the TV on, but with no volume. I just watched until I fell asleep on the couch.

CHAPTER 9: TOP TALENT IMMIGRATION

The next morning, I woke up after my wife had left for work. I could not figure out if it was because of my weird sickness or something else, but I kept seeing black spots around my eyes and peripheral vision. I'd had this before, but now it seemed to have multiplied one hundred times. Every time I opened and closed my eyes, the black spots were appearing at the sides of my vision and then disappearing instantly. I tried not to pay much attention, hoping it would go away by the time I'd had some breakfast and coffee. I couldn't help but moan even more now.

If I were rich, I would have had access to the best diagnosis and any appropriate treatment from the first day of my symptoms. In my reality however going to the public hospital, was only going to get me to a minimum 4 hours wait in the lobby and then straight to the pharmacy after that, to get some painkillers, that would have been prescribed to me by the 'experienced doctor'. This is the reality for a large number of people living in the so-called developed countries around the world and it is sad to even think about it.

Our world is richer than ever before in a very well-constructed evolution time frame, where capitalism never takes so much as a day off from making the world more unequal and subsequently unstable.

My moral high ground necessitates me to ask, why in this richer than ever world, there are more poor people than ever before?

While skyscrapers flourish, the poor neighborhoods expand on the other side of the cities. Refugees hiding behind bridges, packed with new cars driving up and down. The oceans are full of huge ships and by the sea people starve or die drowning in sinking small boats while illegally trying to immigrate to an even more uncertain future. But what do we do, us, the pretentious 1%, who turn to the side in our utopic bed and continue our sleep, while many others literally sleep in the cold, while experiencing constant starvation?

Of course, we are the social class serving the rich. Considering that the systemic capitalistic society we live in, is made by the rich to serve the rich, one of the most valuable income sources has been proven to be worldwide immigration. Have we ever thought that the capital per head leaving the birth land and moving to the richer country to find their luck, collectively and in the long term accounts for 1/5 of the profit, this rich country will make from all of those any type, age, or sex 'refugees', a figure we cannot even comprehend, when it ranges in the trillions per 'developed' country! And that might be one side of the coin. What about the 'quality migrants'?

How many leaders of the developed countries consistently come forward to say, we are welcoming top

talent from all other countries to help our progression and innovation.
What does this mean in the crude reality?
Top minds cannot find work in their home countries.
How come?
Simply because most of those poor countries have been consistently hoodwinked from the same developed countries, so they can snatch the top minds, having them doing the hard work, for the rest of their life and for peanuts!

The poor, the rich and powerful all are connected. Bureaucracy has been developed particularly to exploit the expense of other to those who created it, since behind every sad life story of poverty there is consistently some form of power responsible. Poverty cannot be decreased by wealth alone, as opposed to that it can be reduced by science, technology, social housing, agriculture, correctly deployed revolutionary movements, correct ideology of the free market, but most of all by taking accountability for all actions, not the ones suiting our agendas only. Any plan should include all of these in the equation, not only the ones that can fit in the equation or the ones that could make the equation work as intended by the few, but all humans that have a birth right to life. And if you think the equation will never fit everyone in, then quit your authoritarian selfish thoughts, flash news, whoever you are, you are blatantly incompetent, and no one will ever tell you in your face.

I have a look outside the window and it's dark. I keep getting those black outs, thinking for hours without even realizing it. Already it's Wednesday night and I don't seem to be getting better. I have symptoms that I cannot explain at all. My brain is firing all those out of the ordinary thoughts one after another. I know where I am, who I am, and I remember everything about myself. However, I keep getting momentary shifts from the actual reality, to another alternative reality of my perception of life and honestly, I have begun confusing which reality is the one I live in. It could be this has something to do with the headaches I have got the past couple of days and I am beginning to feel worried. I switched on my laptop to browse new pages. I was hoping that someone might have recorded something similar to what I am going through, feelings and occurrences. I always thought that movie scripts come from real events, even if they are presenting them as science fiction. What I have been going through the past few days is real for me and that makes it as serious. I have to keep looking online for anything really.

CHAPTER 10: SIMULATING NORMALITY

Searching book libraries, online pages, but also real discussions made available to everyone from journalist researchers, as well as a handful of major contributors to this capitalistic era we live in, provides insights to the possibility we live in a computer-generated simulation.

If this by any chance is true, how could we confirm it? The short answer is, 'we cannot'.

As many in the relevant technology fields would support, even if a variable in this simulation changes and we are for some reason able to catch it, what are we going to do about it afterwards?

Most likely we will just stand there like ancient statues and think without a return from it, what the heck was this?

Eventually we realize that all our efforts to understand the fundamentals of nature, slowly but steadily lead us to equations, similar to what drives online search engines, browsers and computing power. Like a website modeled to emulate the planet and everything within it! If we can comprehend this fact, then basically the possibility of our creation as human race to be random is majorly decreased.

Well, considering that the past is allocated memory, the future is another executed scheduled thought,

both occupying space of our present, then the reality could easily be reprogrammed, where the language is a virus, the religion is an operating system and the prayers freaking spam. We humans could be merely deleted items in a virtually created world.
So, do we live the present time at all?
Just think, do you always think over the shoulder of the present about what will happen tomorrow, the following months, year and so on?
Most likely you do, multiple times per living day! What you end up achieving is chopping and shrinking your life up, not living the beautiful today and yes, it is your fault.

When in the beginning of the 21st century you have physics currently working on models of an 8-dimentional crystal, that projected to a 4-dimentional crystal at a specific angle, forming a 4-dimentional quasi crystal, which at the end a 3-dimentional quasi crystal can be derived, while you and me are trying to make a living, the fact we might be living in a simulation is the least of my worries. There you go then, this thinking pretentiously out of the box for most of us, is just an expression that we use from time to time to show off.
It tingles my senses when freaking news hit my ears and eyes, that some of the richest on Earth, as well as some scientists, philosophers and executives of the business world, believe that there is a higher than a 20% chance that we already live in a virtual computer-controlled simulation world. The hilari-

ous fact is that they claim, there are available funds to get humanity out of it!

How can I not ask myself, why they like to mess with our life in so many different ways?
On the other hand, amazingly enough with technology approaching the creation of photorealistic 5-dimensional simulations, in which millions of people can participate simultaneously, it cannot be completely excluded. Given the current advances in artificial intelligence, virtual reality and the power of computers, the members of future cultures may one day decide to create a simulation of the world of their ancestors, i.e. us!

Let's hold that thought and consider for a second, that if this is true, none of us will ever know, except if we feel this 'déjà vu' more often that we should!

Do I mock myself thinking about such scenarios?
Are the 'elite' mocking their own valuable clones, hence us?
Are the creators of our world simulation mocking all of us or are we exercising the natural human habit, whatever we cannot explain we call it God and as we evolve, virtual simulation?

To ease my mind, I keep thinking that in some ways, the virtual simulation matrix is alive in our everyday life. We are 'it'. We keep it alive with the usual actions we do every day, our preconceived notions and expectations that color our world. Just bear that thought for a moment. How often do we ask our-

selves, 'what is happiness and what having fun really means?'
If one can answer this question with proof, then good for them! Have you ever thought, how many people around us cannot answer this question properly and don't be surprised, if most browse the Internet to search for an answer!
The most worrying fact is that the majority of the people on planet Earth, believe that it is normal to live like we currently do and many of them like it also. Scary fact! Whoever tries to noticeably even nudge outside this sleepwalking mode of existence is labeled an activist, to put it lightly.

There you go, it's already Thursday night. Last time I checked it was Wednesday night. Where was I during the last 20 or more hours?
How the heck did I miss Thursday morning and midday, uncontrollably daydreaming. Enough is enough, I am definitely sick from something, but I don't know what it is. Better I get to sleep early and try to put my mind at ease, because fire in my brain is the only way I can describe how I feel this evening. I went to bed, hoping that my biological clock will know that it is time to sleep.

CHAPTER 11: WHAT AM I TURNING TO?

I had already been in bed for an hour and my mind was going crazy. At some point I got up, for some unexplained reason I could hear lots of noise in the room. I opened my eyes, expecting to see the source of that noise in my bedroom. The noise was like metal clinging with heavy bass echoes.

I looked over the covers and nothing was there, but still the noise in my ears was immense. I got out of bed, rushed to the living room to go and look outside the balcony door, just in case it was coming from outside. No one was there. Where all this noise was coming from, I had no clue. Something was far from right. I looked at my feet and they looked kind of swollen and my hands were a bit darkish, like I had bruised them. If this was not a heart attack, what could it have been? I ran to the mirror to look at my face. I looked closer but immediately stepped back. I looked again, closer. I looked back just in case there was a reflection. I was alone in the house, no sources of exposed electric power or lights were on. I looked for a third time closer into my eyes in the mirror. I could see something that looked like a flare moving upwards in both of my eyes. I got closer to the mirror and I could see it clearly. Both of my eyes were literally on fire without feeling any kind of burning or melting in any way that was hurting me. For a moment I began thinking I would explode. I felt like crying but immediately tried not to cry, because I could not predict what my tears would be like! I ran to the living room again, where there was some space to kneel.

I kneeled, closed my eyes and felt like I wanted to pray. I realized that I didn't know any prayers to say. I stayed there with my eyes closed and kept saying, I am sorry God, forgive me for anything I have done wrong, forgive me! I kept mumbling the same thing again and again. The burning and swelling in the body were getting worse, regardless of my hopeless worshiping to God. I could never even remember, if I had worshiped before. I got up and leaned towards the balcony door to look if anyone was outside. It was nearly after midnight, no one was there. I opened the balcony door and stepped out. The first terrifying feeling was that I could not feel the cool night breeze at all. Something was inside me and it was growing by the second. I walked left and right on the small balcony, trying not to make any noise and wake my neighbors, while I was burning from top to toe, inside and out. This had to end somehow. I jumped off the balcony onto the pavement by the road and began walking towards the park adjacent to the other side of the road. I kept thinking, if I die in a weird way, what would happen to my wife, my parents and friends. I reached the entrance of the park and climbed up the fence over to the inside of the park. I walked towards the open green area of the park. I had the feeling that one-way or another I was going to die soon, while making some kind of a mess and wanted to avoid messing up our belongings in the flat or the surrounding area. If I was going to explode or something, I had to be far from any place with people. I reached one of the benches in the middle of the park and sat down. I was not feeling cold, even if it was nearly zero degrees Celsius out there. I was stunned when I realized that I had been barefoot all that time and with my pyjamas. I kept asking myself what is going on with me but had no way to answer that. I was scared, sad, but most of all regretful for all the things I hadn't done during my life. Oh, that feeling was making me so sad. I wanted to have a family with kids, to travel, to experience new flavors, meet new people, play sports, games. All of these were now looking like an unfulfilled dream.

Suddenly, the noise inside my head stopped and this gave me some hope, just before I looked down at my feet and saw the skin on my feet changing from normal to flame yellow. What had been going on inside my eyes, was now starting to develop on the rest of my body. It was looking like the burning flames were growing everywhere on my body. A bit of anger started to kick in. I began thinking about the possibility of the government monitoring my telephone calls, having placed bugs in all sorts of places, deciding that my anti-capitalistic beliefs pose a threat to the overall system. The damn spooks infected me with a lethal toxin, which would burn me to the ground without leaving any ashes. Within this time of despair that I was going through, I found some mo-

mentary space to smile at that thought.
Who did I think I was and if any government would even bother to check even my name?
Then I started thinking that an alien form had infected me with something and that was the beginning of wiping out all humans off the planet. I felt kind of shy calling people in the middle of the night asking them if they had any symptoms!
There was no reasonable explanation to what was happening to me. By the time all those thoughts crossed my mind, the flame appearance on my feet had gone up to my knees. I could see the bright flame, light over the bottom of the pyjamas I was wearing. It was time to accept the inevitable. I would burn to ashes and the few moments I had left, I had to reflect. I sat down on the bench again, like it was a normal night at the park, crossed my legs and looked up at the sky, which was obviously as dark as it could be. I looked back at the natural appearance of the park, the trees and the green.

It all seemed so peaceful and still. I smiled. Life is amazing and only when it's coming to the end, a person truly appreciates it. I was at that point. I couldn't believe myself, how I was so calm when I knew death was minutes if not seconds away. Possibly, this was the calmness you get when the inevitable is about to happen. Accepting the final ultimate defeat, death. I tried to remember my school years, my parents and couldn't leave out my ex-girlfriends. Oh, some were so sexy. My thoughts were interrupted, I couldn't

help it and I looked down at my body again. The flame color was being somehow absorbed by my body. It wasn't burning me anymore and it seemed it was going everywhere over and then inside my body!
I had to move. I got up and tried to sway my body, like I was trying to shake the flame color off me. No luck! During the following seconds I stood and checked all visible parts of my body. Within a minute the color disappeared in my body and I was looking normal, if I could really say that. If this was a dream, it was as real as it could get. I made my way slowly back home. On my way I was looking all around to see, if anyone was there looking at me. I was alone. One thing was strange. The physical energy consumption I was experiencing every time I was walking, was simply not there anymore. The emotional energy was though. And I was feeling drained. I was close to home. I walked in and felt so happy that I was still alive. I didn't know though, if soon I was going to turn to a vampire or a zombie, so my happy thoughts were moderate for the time being. I decided to have a shower and chill out a bit. In the shower another strange thing happened. I couldn't feel the water at all. I tried turning it too hot and then too cold. Nothing! It was like my body was dead. My skin was feeling a bit tenderer, but nothing to indicate that I was turning into an alien. Then, there it was again, the butterflies in my stomach were coming and going. I finished showering and went to sit on the couch. There was nothing else to do. I sat on the couch and tried to close my eyes, hoping I could sleep. Big mistake. Once my

eyes were closed, I could hear the faintest whisper. After I opened my eyes, I could smell the trees from the park across the road from inside the flat. All my senses were so enhanced. I was turning into a vampire for sure. I had all the symptoms. All series and movies with zombies and vampires couldn't all be our imagination, it was happening to me! I got upset again thinking about it and went out of the flat again and from the small road opposite the park I walked to the main road.

It was going to be sunrise soon. It was Friday and I was out on the road walking like a lost cause. If I didn't have enough troubles at this time, there it was, a police car patrolling was approaching. If anything, that was the least I needed now. I was the only pedestrian on the road. I had to pretend, all was normal, so I kept walking straight pretending. The familiar but terrifying sound of the police siren went on, eou eou, beep beep and again and again. I stopped walking and turned my head towards the police car, with a big smile. By now the police car had stopped next to me and the coppers said to me:

"Mate, is everything alright?"

Now would they believe me, if I said to them what was really going on with me or was it going to be a swift pick up and straight to the nick?

"All good officers, I had lots of curry tonight with my mates and couldn't sleep, so I am walking it off", I replied with certainty.

Both coppers nodded and the same one replied:
"I see, well I must say to you mate, you look radioactive, are you sure it was curry?"

There it was, he had me by the balls now.

"No officer, I can assure you I never tried radioactive in my entire life?"

I replied with an evasive tone and immediately thought, hold on, do you think they would take that as an offense, if I mess with them now?

Both of the coppers got out of the car and approached me. The other one says to me:

"Lad, your head is glowing, like you have a lamp in there. Has something happened to you?"

What was that all about, I thought for a moment and looked at the glass window of the police car. What on Earth was that, my head was glowing like I was radioactive for real, which I knew that night I was. I turned my face towards both of the officers, smiled, swallowed my last spit left in my throat and replied:

"Officers this effect was amazing and didn't want to remove it. I was at a trance party last night and got that make up paint on my head that illuminates with light. Looks good hey!"

They both got closer and the same one says to me:

"Well it does look so realistic glowing like that, I will

give you that mate."

The coppers, poor people, once more fooled even by me the most nobody of all. I smiled at them both again and said goodnight. As I was walking further away from them, I could feel that they were still staring at me, but I kept walking like a pretentious, nothing had happened to me person!

A little bit further down the road I changed direction and began walking back home, I could see my head glowing in every parked car window on the side of the road, how the heck didn't I notice that earlier. Soon I was back home, starring at the mirror. What was happening to me?
How could I go into the outside world again with my head looking like a nuclear reactor?

I sat down and closed my eyes. Big mistake again. Usually closing my eyes was dark, this time though I could see pure white and bright yellow colors. I opened my eyes immediately and this was the first time I felt a bit angry. What the heck was going on?
Piss off spooks, I shouted out loud and got up, walked toward the balcony door, opened it, walked out and felt like punching the balcony metal bar. I did! Bang, a strong punch with my right hand on the horizontal metal bar.

And that was the moment changed everything in my life…

The metal bar, that even a car crashing into it would

not bend, with one punch almost broke like a feather, bend like I had smacked a piece of paper. It was so damaged, it looked like a grenade had exploded on it. God and the noise were so loud. If I hadn't woken up all my neighbors with this loud bang, then they had a hearing issue. I stood still and kept looking at the damage. I felt nothing on my hand.

My God what am I? I kept thinking.

I looked left and right, but no one seemed to be out looking. I leaned down and tried to straighten the metal bar. Gosh I could do it, like it was a plastic bottle. I kept squeezing the metal bar left and right, until I made it kind of straight again. I look around again and rushed back into the flat.

CHAPTER 12: A CHANGE IN A LIFETIME

This was something I had to assess fast. Was I super strong? Why? How? Oh, no. Please, help.
I had to calm down before I could decide what to do.
I am nobody, how could this happen to me?
I kept asking myself but at the same time, I had started accepting the reality. I was something else and possibly "nobody" was not that much of a representative description anymore.

It was daytime and I could hear the traffic building up outside and my neighbors upstairs getting ready for work. I knew that with what had gotten into me, there was not even a single chance I would be able to go to work anytime soon. And minute-by-minute I cared less and less about that. My life as I knew it, was now on the line, so quickly enough I was realizing that I had to think about my family and my wife. But before all that I had to get to the bottom of what was going on with me. As time was passing, the burning feeling in my body as well as the radioactive look of my head were slowly wearing off.

I sat down and wrote a letter to my wife and family, just in case I was never going to see them again. I tried my best to explain that something had gotten into me. I made it clear how much I loved them and how proud and privileged I was to be a part of their life. It was funny that even with the immense power I had, my feelings and logic were still intact. After I wrote the letter, I got dressed, put on a hat and looked out of the window to ensure no one was there. I walked out to my car. I got in and started driving to the most remote place I knew. It was about an hour's drive away. I was a bit hesitant to try anything, remembering what had happened to the metal bar on the balcony. I was wondering if I made a sudden move inside the poor car, I might have broken it in two. As I was approaching a large cornfield, I noticed that my vision was not only better, but I could literally see as far as someone could have seen with binoculars. The clarity of my vision had also improved to unreal levels. By now I wasn't as surprised as I had been just a few hours ago. I was actually even expecting more bodily improvements to kick in.

I found a place to park the car and got out. With this unbelievable new ability to see far away, I was able to look more or less a few miles away and make sure that no one was there. I walked towards the middle of the cornfield and tried to pretend that I was an innocent bystander. As I was standing there, I thought, now what?

There was very little to see or experience, if I still had this unexplained immense power in my hands. I decided to jog. Normally I could only do 1 minute and then I would have to take a break. I began running slowly, then a bit faster and suddenly I found myself in another small town!

God, what had just happened now?
I had run for less than three seconds and covered more than 30 miles! Fortunately, I had ended up in an area that was also remote and without any people looking to witness my running like a thunderbolt. I tried to think, was I able to look around while I ran? Gosh, I could! I remember that my brain was like firing a jet engine and had memorized all the places that I was able to run past. Deep inside me, I had started to like it a lot. What the heck was happening to me and most of all, why me?
Without much delay I ran again and again, realizing that I was now somewhere in the middle of the country at a place without any signs. It looked like I was in the Midlands. Feeling so strong and fast and after seeing so many movies of super powered humans without much hesitation, I did the next best thing that anyone would do. I jumped upwards! Wow!
In seconds, I was seeing the whole country from so high up that for a moment I felt butterflies in my stomach. God! I could even fly! The main issue was that I kept going up higher and by now I could see the whole Earth and yes, it is round, for whoever still argues about that!
Scary for a first-time experience because as I kept soaring upwards with unprecedented speed, within seconds I had reached what I suspected was outer space. I was now in deep space, but one thing I hadn't tested was how to go back down again on top of being able to breathe. However, there wasn't much time to have second thoughts and I did what I have

seen in several movies. I used my thoughts to control my body strength and movement. Like I was a natural, momentarily, I stopped flying away from Earth. I think I was near the Moon by the looks of it, floating like a freak, no other way to describe the feeling. My main aim now was to go back. I began flying back towards Earth again and it seemed all was under control. On my way back I even slowed down a bit, to have another look at this majestic planet from above. It took me less than a minute, slowly flying to Earth again and soon enough it felt like I had done it many times before. My body had adjusted to something not even seen before in movies. I was pretty much an improved version of a superman. Once I touched down, I realized that the place I had landed was not that familiar. This was not a midlands cornfield in England but looked more like Antarctica. Actually, it was! I also noticed that I was still dressed in my hoodie and jeans, lost the hat though. Since I was here in the Antarctic, I wanted to test what the feeling would be going underwater. I flew to the nearest seaside and plunged straight into the freezing cold water. I kept pushing further into the water until it was dark. Within less than 5 seconds I was so deep that I even felt a bit lonely. At no point did I feel like I needed oxygen or experienced any other kind of discomfort. I made my way up to the surface and flew back to the icy coast. I stayed there for a bit, reflecting. And then it hit me fast. What if I had been caught on all the radars and military satellites, while I was browsing away in the sky and outer space? What if a mobile phone camera had caught me running from one town to another or when I flew up off the Earth?

I looked down, then up, and I smiled. A geeky thought ran through my mind, let them see me! What could they do, sue me?

With a smile on my face, I flew towards what I thought was going to be England and soon from high up I saw the land structure resembling the whole country, as I remembered it from the maps and flying a little bit to the left and to the right I managed to land nearby, where I had left my car. After I landed, I looked at my poor, tired looking car and laughed out loud, thinking: 'What the heck do I need you for now?' I couldn't believe myself, but I got back in and decided to drive back home! Very soon I realized that the keys for the house were nowhere to be found. I must have dropped them either near the Moon or Antarctica or maybe in the deep sea. Although it was only going to take seconds to reach either place, I thought I'd try something else. It seemed like this was the last time I was going to use any kind of 'human' transportation, so why not experiment a bit, to see how my new superpowers could be used. I went and sat in the driver's seat like I was going to drive the car and closed the door. Then I used my flying power to push the car from the inside and making it look like I was driving like all the others. For a second it seemed it was going to work, however when I tried to stop, the seat broke, jerked backwards into the back seats, which also broke and made a bend in the car that reached the fuel tank, which of course within a second, ignited! The car was on fire and I was still inside it, holding the wheel in my hands, pretending nothing had just happened. I got out and I ran around it to create a flow of wind to try and put the fire out. It didn't work, instead I created a small cyclone and the car was in a second five-ten feet off the ground on fire. I stopped and it fell back on to the ground again this time in several different pieces. I had managed to destroy it completely. Fortunately, I wasn't near any houses or flammable objects, so I started walking away like nothing had happened. On second thought I ran a bit faster, which meant I was near my flat within a couple of seconds. I went in, sat on the couch, closed my eyes and with a wide smile on my face started feeling that all the weird feelings had gone. I felt normal, only with newly acquired superpowers. I had managed to adjust overnight to such an unnatural change in my body. I was positive I had superpowers, better than all the fictitious superheroes combined. Best of all it was all a reality and not in a movie!

As I sat there, the first thing that came to mind was to call the police. I couldn't believe that I would do that, but it was additional evidence of the level of brainwashing we all have from society. Regardless of my newly superpowers acquired, I called the police to report the car stolen, so when they found it, they would not knock on my door and charge me with negligence, but instead they would call me to say they found it burned and they were investigating.

It was already early afternoon on that one of its kind

Friday. I grabbed a pen and a piece of paper. I had to plan my next steps carefully. This thing was happening to me for a reason. Even if it didn't, I had to make it count. I started making notes of the important points I had to consider.

First of all, I didn't know how long these powers would last. At the same time, I needed to test my powers a bit more. There were many aspects of these powers that I might have still not discovered. Second of all, for as long they lasted, no one should know. Then, I had to make sure that I secured my future before I lost the powers. This was tricky since it meant getting money by using my powers. This idea was against all of my lifetime principles. I was constantly witnessing the strongest doing this to the weakest and I didn't agree. The third priority was supposed to be the first one. I had to find a way, to do what all without exception super 'supposedly' heroes in all movies have not done. To help the human race for real, the most weak and vulnerable and never take orders from the powerful.

God, I had only this great power for a few hours and I was starting to feel overwhelmed already. One major thing that I had to keep in mind, was that I was still nobody. And all-around planet Earth, there are almost seven billion nobodies similar to me, who would have loved to feel even for a day or a week like I now feel, a nobody with enough powers to take over the whole world.

Just in case all of this was just in my mind and with a

short expiry, I called my manager at work. A typical move for a common nobody, like me. I explained to him that I had to be absent for another few days, taking unpaid leave due to some family issues. Already my superpowers were costing me money! He believed me and there it was, I was on leave until the day my wife would come back next week, Wednesday. Then I called my wife and told her I was feeling better and there was no need to go the doctors, since I would be returning to work on Monday. She sounded relieved. The phone call went on fine, she told me her last couple of days of events at work, and we said we would talk over the weekend. The rest of the family were far away, for the time being I would leave them as they were, the less they knew, the better!

Before I decided what to do with my powers, I had to find a way to hide my identity. I went straight to the Halloween box we had in the closet. I looked in and soon I realized, that I couldn't be flying around in a cuddly tiger suit, neither in a priest's costume. Bummer! I had to find something that was a bit more serious but also convincing. There were way more important things to try and figure out and I was spending time on what I was going to wear. On the other hand, I knew I had to be covered. One picture from anyone would be enough, for the police to say the least or even the secret service agencies to be knocking at my door, with all that face recognition software they have nowadays they would find me in a few hours.

As I was rummaging through the Halloween box, I

found a very old vintage mask that covered the eyes, nose and most of the mouth. I put it on and looked at myself in the mirror. The first thought that came to mind, was to laugh a bit, but then I thought, what the heck, I am not going to model on television!

I found a dark blue builders' suit with a zipper up the front. I wore it and I put on the mask. I had a quick glance in the mirror, and I thought for a second that yes, I don't only look like a psychopath builder that is out there to cause mass panic and eventually harm, but I also had a bit of a round belly showing. How the heck can someone have superpowers and still have a chubby belly?

I soon overcame these insecurities and opened the door, walked outside the main building and before anyone could see me, I was off running with speed of light towards another remote location. In less than a few seconds I was in the north of England. I was on top of one of the hills overlooking a small village. It was amazing, the fact I was running so fast and could still see everything, avoid hitting objects or causing havoc in the areas that I passed through. I took a minute to look at the very nice view. And then it hit me. That's how I was going to make some serious money and without taking advantage of anyone, as opposed to that, I was going to provide an amazing service. I would become a transport medium for people who wanted to travel from one place to another, way faster than a train, car or an airplane could. I would make an online application form, where people could fill in their details and depending on their income, I would charge them accordingly. The poorest would be able to travel fast and super cheap, whereas the rich pricks would have to pay top buck. I had to ensure this could work though.

Not very far away I could see a flock of sheep, eating carelessly! I ran there, grabbed one sheep and off I went running towards the south of England again. It took me another 3-4 seconds to reach Cornwall. I arrived at an amazing seaside with unbelievable views of the Atlantic Ocean. I put the sheep down and I was waiting to see what it was going to do. The sheep was still alive which was great news. I wanted to see how long it would take for the sheep to adjust from such an intense trip. However, it didn't even take a few seconds, before I could hear a very healthy, "beeh beeh beeh" and the sheep leaned its head back down and started looking for something to eat. I was so happy. I could carry another living organism at almost the speed of light, and it would come out of it completely unharmed. Of course, I had to test it on humans as well! I thought, if I were to explain the business idea to my wife, she would want to take a trial ride! I took the sheep back to the rest of the flock and it was like nothing had happened. It was a privileged sheep and all the other sheep knew that, since once I left it, all of them went close to ensure all was fine. Lots of happy "beeh beeh beeh" was my cue to fly off for another space travel. Once again within seconds I was in outer space and could see Earth from so far way. Oh, it was an amazing view, way better than I could see in photos or television. Very soon two

different pictures caught my attention. As I was flying with moderate speed all around Earth outside the atmosphere, I began realizing that there was space garbage everywhere. This was something that made my overwhelmingly happy mood change. I mean, look at those morons, they screw up the planet with garbage and like that was not enough, they also ruin the periphery of the planet with space garbage as well. Why are our leaders so careless both on the planet and outside of it?
What do they know that we common humans don't, that justifies such actions?
I felt immense frustration but fortunately for some reason, it was not building up as much as previously, almost like my powers had an internal switch to prevent me from getting overly angry. I felt relieved that I couldn't get very angry.
I kept floating mainly across the periphery of the planet and I couldn't avoid noticing a weird color on different areas of the earth's surface. There were many colors that I could explain, like the green of the forests, the blue of the sea as well that darkish grey, possibly a sign of pollution, but there was a dark yellowish towards red color that I couldn't figure out quite what it was. It caught my attention because it was in strange areas spread all over the world, at least that's how it looked from that far away. I had to find out. I began descending towards one of those locations, trying to maintain a course that would land me straight above it.
As I closed in, I got a first hint. It must be a nuclear

power station. Yes, that is what it was. Clearly, I was now less than a couple thousand feet above and could see the whole set up. Without a second thought, I knew I had to test if this was my kryptonite! I flew in, had to break a small metal door, the alarms went off straight away and ran towards the area in which I had seen the strongest color of nuclear power concentration in this complex. Within another huge room there was a large enclosed area, which I had to break in another couple of doors in order to enter. There it was, a huge pool of water with many thick metallic bars immersed in it. Gosh, that was a lot of nuclear power in one place. I jumped in the pool, rubbed myself on those containers, opened my mouth, licked them with my tongue, touched them for an extensive few seconds and off I went. On my way out I could hear the whole complex was on red alert, they knew there was a breach of security, but couldn't find how or what it was that had breached the facility. I flew off and I realized I was above the European continent. I didn't care which country I was in. I was however curious, to see what and if they were going to say anything on the news the next day. I flew back towards England and landed like nothing had happened nearby my flat. I walked towards my flat, after I had taken off my mask, I walked inside like any other normal day!

I sat on my couch and smiled, since that last visit was literary a radioactive move! Soon the smile faded from my face though. It occurred to me that my flat might have been contaminated with nuclear residue, including all the handles of the common doors in the complex that we all lived in leading to my flat. Gosh, I had to run like a maniac again. I went out to look with my super vision on all the areas I had touched walking towards my flat again. There were no visible colors like the one I was able to see from high above. I figured out that what secondary transfer means for all humans, for me was simply not applicable.

Wasn't it amazing? Yes it was! To understand what was happening to me, I would have needed all kinds of biologists, a dozen of astrophysicists, several chemists and physicists to say the least. And this only to tell me at the end, I have superhuman powers! Duh people, I already know that!

After this moment of wisdom, I got back to my normal thoughts. As time was passing it was evident that I didn't feel hungry, tired or sleepy at all. I could fly, dive, go to space, remain unaffected from nuclear radiation while all my instincts, beliefs and pretty much all of my personality characteristics remained the same as always have been! This was better than any superhuman I have seen in movies and without a script to follow.

It was becoming clearer by the minute, there were two big questions:

How long I would be like that and how should I use my powers for the greater good?

CHAPTER 13: USE OF IMMENSE POWER WISELY

Since even before humans existed, whoever or whatever had the most power ruled. From the era of the dinosaurs throughout the primitive emergence of humanoids to ancient humans and then the Middle Ages until today, power meant ruling to the extent anyone can rule. The important difference with my case is that all rulers, had a location reach limitation, coupled with an earthly make up, both of which attributes made them short lived, as well as having a narrow reach throughout the planet. No one has conquered the entire planet Earth for a few simple reasons. Time for transportation has always been an obstacle, the impact and level of strength of their army and eventually biological death.
Those are issues I don't have, except the short-lived part of it for which I had no clue how long I would have these powers for, as well as the possibility of being or not mortal anymore. Those were the main uncertainties I had for now.

I remained all afternoon and evening going into Friday night and after midnight thinking, talking to myself out loud, about what would be the best way to go forward using my powers. Steadily but surely, I was getting there.

I began working on the question of how long my powers would be there in reverse. What if I had opened my fast transport business and after a week or month my powers went away? Busted.

Most likely several government agencies would have been chasing me in order to examine me, meaning simply too much hassle. It was going to be unlikely they would check me for a week and then they would say to me, ok sir, thank you very much, off you go to your morning job as before. Opening a business was a risky approach from every angle that I was thinking of it.

Then using my powers to rip off a few banks that have legally but immorally stolen money from all people for centuries, would have made me the same as those imbeciles, so this approach was a no go for sure.

I also thought about going out there and becoming the vigilante of the reckless powerful leaders. Rip them off and pass all the wealth to the poor. Soon I realized this approach works only in movies and even there, some good people get harmed, if not die. Poor people are used to being poor and the majority of them are proud humans, both are attributes that could lead them to refuse my offerings of wealth to them. Firstly, because they might say, we simply don't want it, don't need it and secondly because even if they accept it, they wouldn't be able to handle the change of their status from poor to middle class and above, just like that. New issues might arise that couldn't be predicted. And on the other hand, I would make several enemies that would try to get to me though harming the poor. It was apparent that I could only predict even less than 1% of the detrimental possibilities of such an approach.

It had to be something else. It had to be something that would make all the wrongs, right everywhere on the planet, forever, independently of my power's expiry date and most of all without any kind of casualties.

I had to use a strategy that would have short transitional stages from how everything works today, to what I will aim the normality for all to become. A small change would not be enough though, it would have to be a large-scale change, that would also last and to do that the powerful would need motives that cannot be second questioned. That was the point of entry for me. I could easily give them the motive! I shouldn't forget though, I am nobody with superpowers and I do have an opinion that is limited to my life experiences and based on the real definition of equality and unified humanity.

It was slowly but surely becoming a plan in my mind. New questions and parameters were arising though. For example who I was going to approach first, in what manner, as whom was I going to introduce myself to, would I allow the rest of humanity to know of my existence and if yes, how was I going to do that, through a TV channel or on the Internet? Too much complexity and I had to sort it out due to the unprecedented time constraints of the fact, I didn't know how long I would be superhuman.

The way forward had to be based on balancing the future wealth equally, by undisputedly motivating the rulers of the planet to make it happen. Knowing that a large number of those rulers are by birth clowns, it would pose a challenge. Surely, I had to consider some would be normal people that worked and became wealthy by serving the community, working for the greater good and never stepped on the backs of others.

The bottom line was, I had to have all rulers in one room, show them that none power of theirs could challenge me, get that part out of the way in a few minutes and then keep them there, make them listen to the view of a nobody human, without having the choice to walk out or turn a blind eye.

It was clear by now due to the fact I had no clue how long my powers will last, I had to find a way to gather all the key players in one place and a way to show up, introduce myself all within the next few hours.

In order to make an appropriate entrance in such an environment without making the world leaders as well as some of the 'elite' feel super threatened, I needed to be considerably well dressed. I went to look in my wardrobe and found a suit I had bought 4 years ago, to go to the funeral of my boss's father. It was pitch black and apart from showing a bit tight on my belly, to my surprise it fit fine. I also had a plain grey shirt and I didn't bother about a tie. It all looked fine on me, so the next step was to find out the place they usually gather. It was already nearly the early hours of Saturday morning. I looked online, since these kinds of questions never occurred to me before. I looked for a few minutes and it was fairly soon that I found the link I was looking for. The leaders of the strongest financially countries, gather once a year to discuss in person, how things are going on with their affairs. That means rulers of countries that have the strongest economies, capitalists that maintain those economies and maybe some of the land sharks that run all of them, but never normally show their faces to anyone, would be there. This was the jackpot, history was craving a new making of itself, since the meeting was due to take place in only two days from today, on Monday! Funnily enough the meeting was taking place in the capital of Greece, Athens, an opportunity for me to visit for first time the place, where everything began!

I tried to close my eyes to rest a bit. Within two minutes I opened my eyes again and felt like I had slept for hours. What an amazing feeling, whatever happens I will never forget.

I then though, I had to see with my own eyes what I was going to fight for, and I wish everyone could have the same opportunity one day. I went out and flew around the globe exploring the natural wonders of the five continents. I was floating over, looking at the panoramic windows of the oceans, mountains, rivers and deserts. I could see humanity revealed in the bright lights of the world's cities. I could see shimmering auroras, raging storms, erupting volcanoes and retreating glaciers. From the lush Latin American forests to the vast African deserts, watery Balkan paradises to ancient Middle Eastern cities, flying over Everest, the Grand Canyon and Victoria Falls, it was literally taking my breath away. All these and many other remarkable wonders were sculpted, etched or molded by unimaginably powerful energies, unleashed by the Earth, reinforcing my motivation to go forward with my plan and constantly justifying the reasons to do it.

Earth is a spectacular place full of hidden and overt beauty in every corner, full of breathtaking sights and each continent has its own impressive locations. Its wonders are parts of the world, that nature has carved on such a scale to simply defy belief. And although for all of us human beings, survival within these extraordinary places did pose great challenges throughout the centuries, it was made possible with our ingenuity.

It felt like a time lapse, the weekend went by very fast, while I was flying all around the globe reflecting on what was to happen. I returned at home later after midnight on Sunday. I checked my phone on which I had several missed calls from my wife, my mother and a couple of friends. I sat on the couch and recollected everything that had happened the last week. I then got up again, got dressed in the funeral suit, waited until it was 6.30 am, the time I am usually up to get ready to go to work and texted them all, reassuring them I was fine and was getting ready to go to work. For first time in my entire life, I was going to do some real work!

CHAPTER 14: MAKE AN ENTRANCE

The biggest Monday of my life was about to begin. It was going to be the day of my contribution to humanity. Who would have thought I would be the 'mate' that would knock the pot upside down?

I left my flat, as always pretending I was going for a walk in the park and then off I went for a swift flight to Athens. It took me just a few seconds to reach a small seaside town, called apparently Porto Rafti and located in the East Attica prefecture which is part of the greater Athens area. I landed on an empty seaside beach and walked for a bit by the sea. That was an amazing seaside place. Lucky people! Further down I saw a couple of locals by the sea, they had their dog running up and down. I approached them and asked about this international meeting taking place in the capital city. They looked at me like I was talking in Klingon language. Either they didn't speak English or they knew what to do for the best, to not care about such unmeaningful gatherings of the 'elite'. Good people. I flew again, towards the Athens International Airport which was nearby and landed behind some bushes, near a taxi queue side road. I walked over to a taxi driver and asked him where this meeting was taking place. He knew, so I jumped in and asked him to drive me there.

It was unexplainable how I still felt butterflies in my stomach. I was by far the strongest man alive and was about to make some unwritten history, but still felt kind of uneasy.

It took him almost 35 minutes to drive me there and he told me that he would have to let me out about a kilometer away, since they had closed the roads for security reasons. I thanked him and paid him with everything I had in my pocket, which was almost triple worth the actual fare. He looked at me, smiled and told me in broken English:

"If you are going in there, make sure you tell them they are all thieves and I am telling you that, because I suspect you are not one of them."

This old man had just made my day. He gave me what I really needed, that one last push. Full steam ahead, swelling with pride and confidence, I was ready to hit this private party.

I didn't know how everything was going to work out, but a way to disable the super tight security without any casualties whatsoever felt simple to me.

It was at least an hour after their meeting had commenced. I had already located the building. It looked like the doors were already securely shut and no one was going in or out. That meant that I could leave all the security on the outside and make my move inside the building. So simple! I knew from a documentary that the acceleration causing human beings

to pass out in fighter jets is the gravitational force experience, when accelerating or decelerating quickly, since a human's blood pressure changes and the flow of oxygen to the brain rapidly decreases. Piece of cake, I made my way in through the roof exhaust tunnel, so fast that none of the guards could see me and then flew in every room of the building with an increasing gravitational force dragging them all around me in the same G force. Within seconds all security personnel were sleeping like babies.
In the conference room I ran in fast all around the main table area, grabbed their phones and all electronic devices up away from them while at the same time I created some kind of gravitational reduction momentarily, so they all were swiped off their seats several centimeters high, before their bums landed hard with a thump onto their seats again. Some screamed, others seemed to enjoy this airy feeling and before anyone knew what had happened, there I was in front of all evil. Without wasting anytime, with a smile and a tone in my voice, I started talking:

"Hello friends! I am sure this was an amazing day for you all, as the last century was. It's only polite for me to introduce myself.
I am Cornelius from an island in the Central Pacific Ocean and guess what, I have superhuman powers!"

A highly 'intelligent' individual shouted from the back:

"Who is this fool, someone call security and what is

going on with the air condition system in here, it's very strong."

Another one shouted:

"Sir, you must be in the wrong room, please walk toward that door and ask security to escort you to the right place, this room is booked."

Clearly, I am a recently made superhuman, so I had to cut some slack to people who felt since birth that their unlimited resources gave them superpowers.
I did what I knew I was able to. I created a wind spin like a tornado entered the room. Within a second, I could see the suits, ties and several shoes together with floating bodies upside-down in the air at least 2 meters high in the room. They were all screaming like little kids on a ride at a theme park. I kind of enjoyed that while it lasted. After less than 10 seconds I gradually stopped the wind spin and one after another were gently landing pretty much everywhere on the floor of the room. I could see the total chaos in there, most of them shouting for help, crying, looking in despair. I had to totally control the room, so I made another attempt to get them focused:

"I hope now I have your full attention. Please, stop trying to understand what has just happened and find your seats, quickly please."

They all walked around the room, scavenging their belongings from all over the place and soon all were sitting, looking as miserable as we all look most of our life. It seemed I was getting somewhere.

"For your information, I am not in the wrong room and no security will walk in that door to save you. I gave them all the morning off! Get used to it because it's going to be only us, uninterrupted for the next few hours. And mark my words, we have lots to discuss. As I said initially, I am the man from next door but with one major difference, I do have proven super human powers that allow me to travel to space and back to Earth in seconds, nuclear power does not affect me at all, I can dig in to the core of Earth, swim to the bottom of the sea and in both circumstances enjoy the ride. I can lift an aircraft carrier with one hand off the sea and leave it back in the sea without anyone on the ship realizing it. I really hope you get the point now.
So, when I say I am superhuman, I actually am a superhuman. Not the superhero geeks you have been presented with in the movies, that possibly one of you has produced and directed, passing the message that anyone with superpowers will also obey the capitalist power. I am the real deal! I mean come on people, making movies that either have a bad guy, that you all will help the superhero to beat or the superhero will beat the bad guy under the directions of the 'elite'! That is a mastermind brainwashing. Well, guess what, we don't want heroes. Because you manufacture them in your movies, doing nothing but obeying the few without questioning a single order you give them. Keep them for yourselves. We are the real heroes, the common people of everyday life. We

have been since day one, surviving from everything you threw at us over the centuries."

They all began mumbling, some louder, others a bit more discreet, creating some uneasiness in the big room. A well-presented gentleman at the back got up and said:

"Mr. Cornelius, just to confirm you are aware that this is not a movie producer meeting, this is one of the most important world leaders and businesses annual summits. We don't produce movies here."

If for a second I believed he was mocking me, I would have honestly decimated him, but I was positive, this was a truthful concern he had. Several others nodded.

"Settle down people, I should say, if I had any common sense, I would have wiped you out of this world once and for all by now, releasing our planet from your corrupt and obviously not that bright minds. But you have brainwashed me so much for almost 40 years continuously, that even if I still feel like 'relieving you from your duties' for good, something stops me. There you go, a superhuman admits it in front of you all, you have won the mind game, you have made humanity, puppets in a theatrical stage for the 'elite' to watch."

A lady at the front of the room raised her hand and said with a loud voice:

"Mr....., we are not all equal in here, surely not from similar backgrounds and most of all without common objectives. I personally never brainwashed anyone in my life and surely I don't view humanity as puppets."

Many seemed to agree with the lady and more mumbling was the only sound in the big room.

"Hold on a minute people. Just come to stand in my shoes for a second and look at yourselves through my eyes. You all look like a happy accident, sitting comfortably all around this room, at the expense of the other 7 billion people that would never get the chance in this lifetime, to simply be half as comfortable as you are. And you say you don't see us like puppets! Damn it, where should I start?

It has been an interesting few millennia, you managed to climb up to the highest levels of human society and made all others kill each other in some way. Well, you might have been a bit too heavy on the political front. Whenever you tried to pay your way to power, you realized simple humans are crazier than you and there you got your civil wars and falling kingdoms. It took you several centuries, but you overcame all that and created, who would think this would work, social media. Everyone now watching videos of cats and sending dick pictures to procreate, so they don't use their brains anymore. Hey and you finally got elections to go your ways with social media as well, so hooray! Then at the same time you took out monotheism with having jihad and crusades, so people find an additional reason to kill each other, for what it is,

the same exact ideology!
And who can say you didn't do some humanitarian work over the last century. Two world wars, way over 100 million people dead, the pie got bigger for you, so you didn't have to deal too early with issues such as the shortage of food, water, housing and energy."

By now they all knew, this was not a joke. I could see it in their faces and hidden fake remorseful looks.

CHAPTER 15: GUIDED HUMAN EVOLUTION

"Let me first set the way this 'summit' will go. I will give you a speech, letting you know my views of the current world status. The view of a semi educated laborer, that simply if he does not work every day, he won't have a place to stay or food to eat. By default, this view represents the majority of the population on Earth, as it stands today. I will provide you with the problems that you might even not know or ever cared about and then I will give you some options. So, you see, I don't really want to have a dialogue with you. If you wanted to dialogue with the common humans out there, you had centuries of opportunities and you never did it. What I want, is for you all to stay here and discuss what would you like to do from now on, after you hear me. Sit back, on those comfortable chairs and enjoy the ride, because it will be one in a lifetime opportunity."

Silence... Finally, I begun getting their attention...

"Humans by nature are greedy, which by default is what all your mass control strategies are based on, without allowing this to become dominant in your ulterior plans, you always knew better than that."

"Superman", another lady shouted, "All human beings

exhibit the ultimate 'addiction' of greediness. Greed offers us an evolutionary advantage, and anyone presented with such opportunity, would take it, no questions asked."

"I can't agree less," I replied, and she sat down with a puzzled face.

"Evolution means change and strikingly fundamental to all of us is trying to understand what an original proposal of natural selection to humans is. We are very similar to all other forms of life sharing a basic biological predisposition, whereas we differ on the aspect of how intelligent we are. We know we exist, something that gives us the grounds for great joy. Notably this always will carry an existential burden, knowing we are here, we also know that someday we won't be here. To remedy those factual thoughts, we constructed the different cultures that throughout the centuries have provided us with different kind of subconscious ways out, to underline the potential of immortality, usually through religion or even by supporting parallel dimension scenarios. Those cultures make most of us want to wake up tomorrow morning and keep doing what we believe works for us. Why do the same fundamental reasons of existence, make you want to wake up tomorrow morning for only one reason, making more money? Do you really believe you will live forever?"

A man looking confused answered, "Well, we have increased the life expectancy significantly over the last century and this inevitably required more money to support us."

"Do you honestly believe this answers the question or justifies any of your actions?" I shouted at him and he sat down a bit scared.

"This neurotic desire of yours for money and greed, describes a person that live their life, consistently seeking and acting upon something that is not true.
An animal will take what they need to survive, whereas the human 'animal' will take whatever they desire and this unquestionably throughout the centuries made you believe that you can think further beyond where any others can think. What do you think makes you so different from all the other humans?
Is it the addiction to your own narcissistic ego?
Do you really think that the richer you are, the more immune to every kind of harm you are?
I keep trying to find excuses for your greediness, something that would make me cut you some slack for behaving like morons for centuries. How are your actions and behavior any different from what the animals in the jungle do to each other, which is simply, dominance hierarchy?
I just cannot justify it, what has happened to all of you, either human brain evolution bypassed you and all your ancestors, leaving you all to be boneheads or you are sick addicts. An addiction with which you have also infected most humans alive at the moment, which is by default a crime against humanity. Most

people alive want to be better than everyone else at everything, even if it is how many hot dogs they can eat per minute. And sadly, I suspect you have done that for your own amusement. You get to be the best by how much money you have and let all the other humans compete against each other for how many hot dogs they can eat.

But still, after so many centuries of doing copy paste for the same crimes to humanity, you disregard the fact that the only thing you gain is depression. You don't have human cultural values anymore, whereas at the same time you cherish values that you are not able to attain."

By this time, many of them had a puppy face, realizing more and more that the end of what they knew for reality was dissolving by the minute.

"I told you, I will highlight the problems and it's only fair to begin with us, common people's share of responsibility. It is our fault taking all that rubbish you fed us, especially over the last few decades. I place this fault, first on myself. Because I am one of those nobodies fed with nonsense all my life and I was swallowing it daily without even chewing it, like most do. I should not have fallen for it and that is my responsibility, I don't blame you for that entirely."

A relatively young man sitting near me throughout, watching him writing down all the time, got up and said, "Sir, I took the liberty keeping the minutes of this somewhat different meeting. I just felt it's notable that this is the first time you don't blame us for something entirely!"

In any other circumstance most would have laughed, but none in that room cracked even a smile! Look at that, I might get something out of all of it today!

"Thank you for this note" I replied, and I continued, "as for all other humans, it's simply sad only to think of it. Scientists, police officers, doctors, soldiers, even some rare found politicians and a list of common people really join this charade of dullards thinking they will make a change. Many of those people tried to make a move against your 'empires'. But I will be naïve not to say, they all have been the key pawns out of the million poor nobodies. Because they always knew, deep in their brain are thoughts in a place no one can go, that whatever they were saying or trying to do, was not going to be enough. They had to go ten steps further to make a real change and almost none of them did. And once the already poorly bribed, manager, principal investigator, army lieutenant, director of the hospital was saying "this is not on our current agenda", all of those cowards were going home, opening a bottle of cheap wine and calling it a night. Without a single exception, all poor human nobodies like myself had it coming and sat there watching our species occupation by the 'elite' unfolding."

I feel lighter already, telling them all off like that. It was cleansing for my soul. I wish all humans were here to witness that.

"You must all know well, as long as there are some of us throughout the different generations visualising how life could have been, we will always have people that will not accept life to be as you like to present it to us.
For much of human history the biggest problem was scarcity. Humans experienced hunger and poverty and this urge to acquire, soon begun going beyond one's basic needs, part of which was based on our human nature. As civilization began to advance, material goods became more available, but still were never what we consider plentiful, except from a tiny minority of cretins, who called themselves what you all call yourselves in here, no need to remind you!

"Mr. superhuman, I struggle to understand a term you keep using and with hesitation I would like to ask you, what is the 'elite' and if you refer to us in here as the elite," a lady from the back said.

"You are the key machinery of the 'elite' and some of you in here could be the 'elite' themselves. For thousands of years there were only few of your own ancestors that were doing the big time consuming, the rich and powerful, who called themselves, kings and queens, rulers and self-baptized gods, put simply, the 'elite'. For all of them the luxury life had a primary purpose. They wanted to distinguish the powerful from the poor, living in a rigidly divided society, where the poor were accepting their fate without a question. They had a secret ingredient, which was used throughout the centuries, the fear of God. Most major faiths have historically stressed the importance of spiritual virtue over materialism and in the past, this was to set the tone for society. What really served your cunning ancestors well, was the church that reinforced most humans' belief to be satisfied with little, leading to seek an eternal life after death not a better life here on earth. So, I now ask you, my lady and the rest in here, are you or are you not the 'elite' or part of it?"

Most looked away, she pretentiously had the look she wanted to reply back, but she didn't.

The stillness in the room was once more my cue to continue...

"But after hundreds of years when wealth and material availability was thrown upon people's hands, everything changed."

CHAPTER 16: SYSTEMIC DOWNTURN

"Only during the last 3 centuries, trading created a new era that some thought it has helped our society further evolve, the creation of the middle class. But soon realized it brought upon us the first few societal sickness signs of self-interested individualism, where the desire for luxury had already begun serving as an economic driver, providing the illusion that everyone can be richer. You could not resist that opportunity, you used that new era of manipulation in the best way possible. Unleashing the unprecedented power of economic growth by allowing individuals to follow their own economic interests, using an economic model that once and for all would have taken over the world, the birth of capitalism."

"I feel the need to intervene here Mr. Cornelius," a tall, chubby gentleman called out. "Surely having experienced 'economic systems' such as slavery, mercantilism, fascism, marxism and planned socialism, capitalism proved to be the most effective way to foster the democratic values of our society."

"And look where we are today", I yelled at him, "congratulations, you have made it an economic nuclear boom. You know more than anyone that the plot has been lost and you know even better that you have no way of putting this genie back in the bottle, ever again. On a planet spanning 58 million square miles of land, you managed to create a one-way road!

You made money to be the new manmade God, which you made to be worshiped by everyone on this planet regardless of their background, culture, age or ethnic group. The result is too obvious to even pretend you cannot see. For every millionaire there are billions of people working to merely be able to live with no other substantial benefits whatsoever and for every billionaire there are millions of people working as slaves. Without ever caring for the fact that all this money you make, has been taken from thousands of people that might need it more than you do!"

Most looked subdued and the chubby man looked under the big table pretending that he lost something, possibly his dignity…

"Your collective empire-ships that answer to no one, take decisions without any accountability for our hard-earned money and you count on the corrupt system in place to bail you out, if things go sideways. You know better than anyone that an economy based on extremes of wealth is not safe. Instead, it is a cartel economy that you feed over and over again. You also know that a society based on unsustainable growth is entirely toxic for most humans.

In less than a century you depreciated the value of all your corruptly made currencies throughout the world with an incredible loss in value that in reality has not been lost, but instead you baptized it 'inflation', so that you can transfer the gains into your uncountable reserves with a mechanism that one of its forms is hidden taxation. A calculated tactic to bring all humans within less than a century and a half to absolute poverty! But that's fine with you.

Keep cutting new worthless paper money, for reasons I bet you don't even know any more. There are trillions and trillions of paper money currencies all around the planet, of which several billions of these are unused in safety boxes and under the mattresses or hidden in walls, in the hands of people thinking that it is some sort of security or that it enhances prosperity and peace!

And you keep up the "good" work, flooding the world with new cut notes, where banks get the opportunity to use this money to make money not by selling goods, but by simply using money to sell money, at a time that all of your capitalistic hungry in power prime ministers or presidents deregulated all the banks, allowing them to rip off all the unsuspecting unprivileged people. Credit cards, privatized public services, pensions cropping, stock market on the rise as never before. A liberalization gambling model for the rich with several distinct failing check points for the poor to pay!

You are consistently using your power to hide your global economic creation within a sick financial system, that large corporations lend money to each other without any kind of regulation. The same corporations then lend this money to other smaller entities, flooding the world with cheap money creating a bubble without cure. A bubble that only the lower classes feel at the time it bursts and look at the history of how many times this has happened.

You have repeatedly bankrupted the middle-class person and foreclosed their assets, which is the only security most of them will ever have. And why was that, to keep nurturing a world system where millionaires are being pushed out from neighborhoods from billionaires. The same billionaires then making cities that its own workers cannot afford to live in, but the greedy, clever rich sharks make more money every day, from fat deals tailored most of the time to negatively impact the middle and lower class. And you put in pretentious new regulations that are in advance agreed with the large corporations, so they can make even more money than before. Even me, the most nobody of all, I know companies that still exist, that have been sold three times the last decade and each time for several million more, each time with loans that never have been paid in full until the other purchase took place, making for each seller more than 700% profit each time! How is it possible the value of those kind of companies go up each time they go bankrupt and the salaries of the people that give more than half of the real value of the company, go down?"

And as if this was not enough, you come out in the open claiming that 'a stronger economy means a stronger planet'.

How criminal is that?

When you make up the ground rules of economics to be based on scarcity, inequality, unequal competition, imperfection, ignorance and complexity, all notions carefully made to make you trillions and you leave all of us, the only notion you don't choose, 'poor luck'.

If this is not how you operate, then why is poverty increasing worldwide, unequally, being at its highest level for the last century?"

CHAPTER 17: THE WORLD PARTY OF POLITICAL PARTIES

It seemed that not even one of them wanted to say something anymore, but before I was to continue my thoughts, a lady tried to save the moment,
"Superman, we have governmental systems in place to monitor the movement of the available capital and ensure tight regulations are in effect to avoid deceitful actions. If some try to bend those rules, within time get caught and penalized. We do have examples of such occurrences."

"Exactly my next point, who did you put to do the dirty job in the center of all this mess, politicians and political parties. All of whom worked so hard to make up the educated laborer and the high school millionaire. It was politicians' bright ideas of fascism, communism, democracy and even the fading nowadays religion, all doing their bit to serve your total supremacy, creating the modern human immersed in 'consumerism', a global language rendering millions of people to call department stores, a 'leisure activity'. Have you ever asked yourselves, what would be the price to pay for this?"

Robbing humanity from reason and good sense and within a few centuries coupled with unattainable in-

equalities, was only the beginning of an unavoidable end of all life. You bully millions of intelligent people to buy more materials every day, making them think they buy something different each time, but at the same time you are selling them one subconscious idea, the more they consume the better their life, growing generations of compulsive shopaholics.
You unquestionably know what motivates our planet's populations and easily influence their behavior without them even knowing it. In almost every act of our daily life, we are dominated by the few of you, because you simply have the understanding and the financial means of controlling the public mind. You have made us believe everything and nothing at the same time, unable to make up our minds about what might happen tomorrow."

"Cornelius" a man got up looking sharp called me out. "Without being rude to any other person in here or to you specifically, I must say that you have given us too much credit. I very much doubt that the majority of the people in this room have a clue about most of the points you have raised, let alone being responsible for implementing or ever carrying out such dominating policies. I just wanted to let you know, in case you are getting carried away based on the audience you have."

"Let me disagree, Mr....," I shouted back at him.
"By being contributors to a system where a single person in most cases, judges or rewards people by their mistakes and not their good actions, does make you

a key subsidiser to all of what you said. It does not matter if someone else told you to do it and it wasn't your idea in the first place. The results remain to be, you did it and your action affects millions. You have given one person all of the power to change the lives of many, even if it has been repeatedly proven to be against the greater good. Prime ministers and religious people sending men to war, executive managers of corporations bankrupting their money laundering 'cells' while destroying the life of thousands of people and also more often than not the cities they live in. Why nothing ever happens to any of them, instead they get to own an island, a yacht or a private jet."

Looking at them while I 'lectured' them, I realized that I didn't know who was a politician, who a corporation representative and if any of them was from the so called, 'elite'. To me, they all looked the same, so I kept on the lesson they all have been absent from, throughout their fake life,

"Most of you in here are at the highest level that any politician can be. I must ask you, do politicians really believe they can make a change that would last and the people who need it the most will really feel it?
I really wonder sometimes, once you get 'elected' and arrive for first time in the cabinet 'hood', how long does it take to receive the envelope with the 'script'? I mean someone in here must be able to answer that, but don't bother. Your actions reflect to what we common people live throughout the centuries. You consistently got your own countries into debt,

because you spend more money than you raise, blatantly, irresponsibly and then you borrow, more than you can afford to pay and as if this wasn't enough negligence and abuse of power, you then print new money and in the end, you ask the poor tax paying civilians to pay the bill for all of the above.

You have the health care in the so-called developed world at its worst of the modern times and for the rest of the planet nonexistent?

How can this also not be another mischievous plan of yours, failing in all public categories and you promote the savior of the century, privatization, which at the same time destroys or fully controls any kind of labor unions, a human right that took years to build, while it you took less than a decade to demolish!"

I remained silent for a moment. I think that scared them more, than even highlighting their crooked actions. Strange, for someone having a bit of ethic in them, insulting your life work unfairly, would make you more emotional, whereas in here I see 'statues'.

"Seeing you in here now, I am sure you think everything I tell you and the way I see the world at the moment is maybe naïve, childish, or even wrong and too emotional. You most likely feel I am too unfair to many of you.

Hold on to that thought for a moment and look at where you brought the world with your policies. We have 99% of the wealth of the entire planet concentrated in 1% of the population. You completely disregard the existence of the 99% and what do you do for the privileged 1% of the population of Earth that do not live in poverty?

You have created something called "the public services" which you offer in each of your countries. What an amazing way to rip off the hard-earned cash of your own people. Health service, civil service and the list goes on and on! Most of these services which are bankrupt or in huge debt, understaffed and unable to deal with the common person's daily issues. You build roads that after a year or so, not even horses could ride down, you concentrate work opportunities in big cities, creating unreasonable demand and subsequently road traffic that people waste tens of hours every week being stuck in. At the same time you consistently refuse to reward the people keeping your own unfair system running, the police officers, nurses, teachers, fire fighters, even the soldiers, all of which are paid peanuts and on the other hand you praise and keep bailing out the rich happy bankers that destroy the global economy every few years!

For several centuries over recorded history we have done whatever you tell us to do, like the poor sheep that go for slaughter, only because you are posing your empire-ships of fascism as political commercialism and we simply fall for it. So yes we hold an almost equal responsibility for the current state of humanity, because even if when we go to sleep at night, we keep wondering is our water and food safe, does our doctor work for our best interests, are our politicians working against us, even if they come out every new election term asking for our support, which naively enough we give them. We then wake up in the morning, we still do whatever you tell us. We take daily psychological manipulation slaps, which over generations have hypnotized us, making us unable to put up an unprecedented fight against this sick norm."

CHAPTER 18: DEMOCRATIC BACKSLIDING

They all looked a bit tired and beat. Some were missing their tops, shoes, glasses and most were a bit dirty. They all looked as anyone would look after they survived a mini tornado. Another good-looking lady got up and said with determination:
"Mr. superman, we live in a democratic society which is work in progress, nothing can be perfect and if you compare it to many other countries that as we are here today, they exercise dictatorships, we are better off for the time being, I should say."

She upset me, because it shows how much brainwashed they are.

"Democratic you say, emulation of dissimilarity we hear with an underlying aim to eliminate meritocracy. For almost a century your predecessors advertised that you would work without rest, to make your countries an equal opportunity for all. Don't dare to tell me that it isn't in those countries in which today exist the greatest divides. The democratic countries!
In an evolving world generation after generation you have managed to make the radical reduction of personal responsibilities possible and at the same time

the legal difference in ethical compensation. When was the last time you asked yourselves, where your democratic official responsibilities are?
I can enlighten you, well maybe they were lost in the impersonal whole, since you never become accountable to anyone. Never got punished no matter what crime you committed to the detriment of the community as a whole. Over the centuries you made the term democracy meaningless, by simply empowering the rule of the majority without clear political goals set for the greater good.

However, once something goes sideways after you have demonstrated a high level of lack of structural memory from your previous ravages, you have the remedy of changing the basic laws of democracy. Any political group that seizes power, can change the educational system, the economic policy, the defensive doctrine, any time in whatever direction it wishes and without any barriers. Who would argue that you present those changes to be for the better, but they are usually for the worst, as modern political history has proven time after time? As with all types of power, your so-called democracies slander pious citizens as religionists, theocratic or ancestorists without curbing for moral decline. You never stopped promoting moral relativism, materialism, whereas at the same time you abhorred the spirit, the collective future, the quality and the moral absolute."

Someone in the middle of the room wanted to talk. A tall gentleman well statured but looked like he had an unsuccessful tan and bleached hair! I wonder. I nodded, welcoming him to get up and talk:

"Mr.… superman, apologies in advance if I am interrupting your colorful speech. I am a professional politician in my country for the past 19 years. I heard you closely all this time. You seem to be talking down to what really matters, if I may say, which is rare in our circles. I can associate with your perception of how everything is currently unfolding in our societies and you do have legitimate reasons to be upset about all that. I gladly want to be the first, to openly propose you come to work for our government, as a consultant."

And there it was, I even got a job offer! Who would have thought, Cornelius from Kiribati would be consulting an entire government, my mum would be so proud! And that is how they are hiring! Their audacity can turn me into a mass murderer.
I looked at him, exactly how my wife looks at me, when I tell her my ideas about moving to live in the woods. In a second he got the message and sat down, being I hope at least humiliated. I continued my 'talk', trying to forget that this just happened,

"When your governments go off the rails with their ego and manipulation, it's down to us, common people, to put them back on to the correct rails with our meager hard-earned money. We have now realized, your governments are derailed and with no brakes. The government protects the banks, the

banks protect your criminal organizations, which all function at the expense of the common human, working his ass over a lifetime to pay the tax, which keeps the crooked system running. By using one tenth of that tax money for our cities and governmental services, you even make us believe that our tax money actually comes back to us common people. What a joke?
Regardless if any of you in here were initially part of this deeply corrupt operation or honestly realized what is going on, once you got 'inside'. Fair enough if you decided you didn't want to be a part of it. But can someone explain please those unexplained deaths and road accidents ending up straight to the organ donor wings of anyone who decided to uncover your corrupt operations, 'the whistle blowers'."

I saw a couple of them looking very guilty. I wasn't surprised...

"You create tax heavens for the rich and make the poor people pay like there is no tomorrow. Even this little bit of hard-earned money that we manage to gain and save, you take it off us. You completely disregard that most people out there have one change to purchase a house or save some money for themselves and the way you have structured the entire global economy, you take that one chance away from them. The way you value one's life nowadays, simply means that money can buy life."

A man got up with a bit hesitation and said, "Mr. Cornelius, most governments represented in this room have policies to provide loans to their citizens with nearly zero interest to buy their first house. We also provide business loans to help the people opening a shop or a small business. In many cases those funds are in the form of grants that they don't have to return them back!"

"Yes, you have done that, but with a long-term plan that is far from the benefit of that poor civilian. You make debt cheap, so we fall for it and borrow. Then we think we can 'leverage' and invest the borrowed money or assets to make a profit. Soon enough after having made debt available to all of us, you pop the fake bubble, sending us all into a life in debt, running like headless chickens to your investment banks, hedge funds and private equity firms for a bail out with triple the debt. You write the rules of the game, so you never lose. You operate the financial markets with greediness that makes you want to take the bigger risk aiming for the higher profit."

By now they all seemed they needed a break from this dominating monologue, but have they ever given us a single break over our entire lifetime?
Let them see how it is to have to deal with someone a thousand times stronger than them without taking a break.

"All these so-called democratic rules you have made available in your developed countries, are like a metaphor of a crook that goes in a shop with a gun and says to the manager:

'Don't call the police, I know the chief of police in the city, he won't send anyone to help you,
Don't try to stop me I have a loaded gun and I will shoot you, and while I steal from you, smile, be good to me, also tell me what the best products are so I can steal quality stuff and I don't have to come back every time to get a better product.'"

CHAPTER 19: EXISTENTIAL MATERIALISM

"I have been trying hard all my life to figure out why you are all so greedy, why you need to have as much money in your hands?
What would be the difference in living a happy life, if you have one 3-bedroom house for your three family members instead of a mansion that can house a dozen people?
Have just one car instead of a collection?
Have a bank account with funds to help you and your kids, instead of money reserves for ten generations down the line?
Why do you need to have clothes that you never wear, whereas others have no clothes to wear whosoever?
Why do you throw away tons of food, when there are others starving?
These questions have no end and there are only a few logical answers.
You must have found the magic pill of eternal life. Well, if that's the case, living for ever requires unlimited funds available. But what makes the 'elite' eligible to live forever and the rest of us not? Try justifying that. Another possible explanation for your uncountable greed could be that you are all vampires and again you will live forever, blah, blah need funds to stir your blood banks the way it suits you. Hold

on, you might also be extraterrestrial beings and the ulterior plan is to consume all the resources of Earth and everything living on it until there is nothing else to exploit. I won't be majorly surprised if you say everything we know, see and feel, is after all a digital world. That we live in an augmented reality and all the mess is due to software glitches. Well, get the software engineers to do their job for a change! But if none of those are true, then why do you gather so much wealth?
Can someone be so addicted to money and power?
Could this 'nuts gene' you possibly carry, pass down so many generations?
Or, what am I missing here?"

Another man at the back got up and with a confident tone in his voice said:
"Honorable gentleman, Mr. Cornelius, I personally believe that everything you said has some serious degree of validity. I must also ensure you, we are all humans in here and life in our world is as real as it can be, maybe that is why it is not perfect at all and possibly never will be! As for being rich and greedy, there are different types of rich, but I would agree only to one type of greediness. I hope you can make that distinction."

For crying out loud, this chap talked but in reality, said nothing. I suspect he is a 'new kid in the hood' and he wanted to show to the others that he can also talk to superman, just for the showoff. He looks similar to the other tanned gentleman tried to hire me earlier, minus the tan. If they are not related, then extraterrestrial it is for them two!

"Mr. honorable whoever you are," I replied to him, "next time you want to say something, say something, don't just get up and then sit down."

The sheer dexterity of human emotion made quite a few in the room show a wistful smile after this comment. They might know something I don't, but who cares, I continued…

"I have never been rich or ever had the hunger to be, because I see life in another way. So, it will take time for me to understand the different types of rich, as well as the greedy. Maybe I would never do, due to my own reality, the inner love I feel I have for life. Life is about love, smells, views, sharing, giving and taking unconditionally, life is a gift that needs appreciating and living, it's like a blooming flower. No matter how many years of life are stolen from the billions of people suffering at the expense of the 'elite', no one can 'bank' those years to use them for their own selves. You will all live more or less the same amount of time.
Have you ever thought how many years we all literally have available since we are born?"

That should not be taken as a rhetorical question. Every human on Earth should know the answer to this question. We should know the time frame we have given to experience life. In this room, either none have ever asked themselves this question or their guilt let their faces, 'blank', no expression whatsoever!

"Let's say you live till you are 90 years old. The first 2 years of your life you eat, shit, cry or laugh after every feeling. Then you begin understanding who is who and what is what until you are 10. For the next 8 to 16 years you are in education believing you learnt everything. Then you find yourself being 26 realizing that in reality you know nothing. Before you know it, you have worked for another 50 years in order to be able to eat and support your family, if you have managed to make one. For some who like their job, they spend 50 good years of labor being 'happily productive', but for those who don't, whoever cared?

Then at nearly 80 years old your priorities once more shift to eating, shitting, laughing and wondering without a reason. With such a lifeline, minus the 30 years sleeping, uncountable days you were sick in bed, psychologically down, commuting or traveling to go anywhere including to work, you end up with less than 5 years of clear free daytime lifetime to do whatever you really want. Five years spread through a lifetime, that's all we really have.

What you consider to be a vast number of choices you made available for our life, is in reality a tiny crumb of options you have left us in a society cut and measured for the benefit of the few.

We are humans and when we do anything that is out of your preset 'norm', we do it because we feel we have no other choice. And let me break out the news

to you, all that does not make us enemies of the state! When was the last time that any of you in here had no other option?
Because if you ask me, I would say every single day of my life, I feel cornered on almost everything I do. Throughout your life you refused to accept that we are all passengers on the same ship, and we are all unique in one way or another."

I stopped talking and I did float upwards in the room to remind them who I was. A buzz went on in the room, both from my hovering and their amazement of the sight. I wanted to test if they had by now, realized the seriousness of the whole situation, so I made a suggestion!

"I have talked for more than a couple of hours. I see you are tired. If any of you feel we need to have a break, please feel free to go for refreshments, we shall recess for 15 minutes."

Unbelievably, I did see several of them getting off their comfortable seats, looking left and right to find a way out.
Was I wasting my time here?
Did they still think that I was another concerned citizen and once I finish this 'unconfirmed occupation' I would make friends again and fly off?
I shouted loudly, creating a tremor in the entire room:

"Are you a lost cause or what?
What did you think? That you would get to have a

break!
Do you still believe this is another of your fake meetings?
Forget what you knew and what you did up until you arrived here this morning. Sit down on those chairs, because mark my words, this is the last time you will sit so comfortably."

Was it my last emotional comment, the earthquake or I had begun to get to them? The mumbling stopped and they all sat down quietly again, looking really scared.

CHAPTER 20: SERVANTS OF TECHNOLOGICAL ADVANCEMENTS

"Like all other mischiefs were not enough, then you come out in front of the beaten public and you say, 'we push forward with cutting edge technology, innovation and science'.
Now isn't that hilarious?
Let's look through the eyes of your ultimate creations, the human nobodies living in a developed country. Let's see how I benefit from all this 'pushing the frontiers forward for the greater good' you have done. Medical research coupled with biology and biotechnology, even a cat would grow intelligent brain to laugh at all those. How did you benefit the masses of common people with any of those, when we go to a doctor for an appointment that takes days to book and whatever we have, the doctor will subscribe us a painkiller and that's it! We still die from cancer in the so-called developed world and mosquito bites in the undeveloped world. By now you know well, we also believe we die from crops, after you made sure we can only buy spores to grow our crops from one company in the entire world.
Which of you had this ingenious idea, controlling the quality of all food at any given time?

"Sir, we haven't got any reports indicating that control of quality of food harms the society on the whole. As opposed to that, we have a way to monitor what we feed on," another gentleman shouted from the back, hiding behind a few others, like I couldn't see him!

"When was the last time you asked the opinion of a real farmer?
When was the last time you consulted a farmer about the kind of quality your transgenic seeds consist of?"

No reply, not a surprise…

"You have one company controlling all agriculture, one company controlling all pharmaceutical production, one company controlling banking and the financing system, one company controlling water and one company controlling oil. All of those companies control all the governments.
You diverted innovation to a handful of drug companies that are serial killers of millions of people, filling them with all sorts of artificial made toxins and fake drugs. Companies that have been pioneers in both major wars in the last century and you know that better than anyone. You keep them running with the immigration scientists, after bankrupting the infrastructure and economy of countries that were doing well or had the resources to do well in the future and made the best brains all over the world, leave their countries and come to work for you for peanuts, in order to fulfill your agenda that has nothing to do with pushing forward innovation for the

greater good. As opposed to that, you use science and innovation for military purposes to demonstrate between you all, who is the most powerful destroyer of life as we know it.

After all of this, how can anyone argue the possibility that one of the key points of the third attempt to conquer the world without weapons is dependency and you are right on track. Before you make people addicted, you make them poor first. You sell us something that is completely the opposite of what it should be, e.g. synthetic drugs, most likely carcinogenic.
How can you make us believe that the basis of the drugs you sell us cure diseases and not create markets for diseases under the umbrella of health care, so you reach your goal faster and more safely?
How is this innovation and pushing forward ethical?"

Some at the back of the room kept looking at each other. Those must be the 'drug sharks'. I was right to say that all sorts of 'upstanding individuals' are gathered in those kinds of meetings! Up until now I haven't picked up on anyone, but those 2-3 funny faces were making me want to make a start…
I behaved myself and before I was about to continue another lady got up with increased airy looks and said out loud:

"Mr. superman, several of your last points are on our agenda. We will improve on those aspects. They take time and, in many occasions, one would begin a project of such importance and it will take one or two generations of scientists and project managers to bring the same project to conclusion. See for example our efforts on the space frontier over the last 50 years or so."

I really laughed out loud and my reply was without remorse:

"Space innovation, isn't that another joke or what?
Not even my second-generation grand kids will have the opportunity to see another planet through even a window of a spaceship that can take them there. You keep spending money on space programs for the last 70 years, to benefit who?
Either you just launder money on something that no one can directly monitor you on or you know we are very close to a total collapse and you prepare for a one off migration to another planet, just in case your 10 miles under the Earth's surface bunkers are not enough.
Do you realize, that in this scenario you will remain in the history of mankind as the 'people' making human beings the first form of life responsible for their own extinction at its peak of evolution!

I keep reading your mischievous attempts to convince common people around the world that planet Earth is overpopulated, that our resources are being depleted and soon we must have the ability to live on another planet in order to accommodate all humans. Stop fooling us so much! Have you ever thought that yes planet Earth is too small for 7 billion enemies, ripping it's guts out daily, but it is way too big for even 14 billion friends? If you respected this amazing place, we all inherited by our birthright, you would have extended its life by another few billion years and many more could easily have lived happily at the same time!

If you are legitimately trying to achieve something in outer space, more than selling expensively satellite communications and Earth surveillance for domination, show us the future benefits, share the exploration process, take us there and make us a legitimate part of real initiatives. Most of all, work together internationally to save time and reduce spending, leave greed and fame out of such attempts."

Her face looked shamed, but that wasn't my intention. Shame won't save the day. Actions and re-direction of current world priorities would! I carried on...

"Hearing the experiences of our grandparents and parents sharing between them two world wars, we expected at the beginning of the 21st century for there to be a hope for a changed future. You see, even if it's a new week, month or year or even a new job, partner, house, we still have hope that something will change in our life for the better.
So what was the highlight of the new beginning you decided to make available to us this century?
After testing its capabilities on your military platforms, you made available the breakthrough of all

communications, the World Wide Web for everyone to use. You made an invaluable tool to be used as the next weapon of mass human control and you make us pay for it at the same time, twice! Firstly, by funding the military to develop it and secondly by paying the internet service providers to use it. I can only assume that you must have rewarded very well the creators of this virus type of control, literally spreading inside the lives of all people willingly using it.
Even to the most unsuspected person it would not be so difficult nowadays to convince them, that the Internet is not there primarily to take our money faster, feeding us your fake news, creating fear faster and keeping track of every move we make constantly."

A man at the front with no top whatsoever, but ripped like a model, got up, showing off a bit and said looking at me:

"Mr. Cornelius, long shot question but I will take my chances. Can you imagine how the world would be today, if we didn't have the WWW available for all? It would have felt like we live in the stone age. Scrutinizing a service connecting humans from all over the world in seconds, it's so unfair for all the hard work put in this technology. You should admit the positive benefits are more than the negative regarding the Internet."

He looked like his key brain neurons had been relocated to his abs, hence his considerations about me slagging the Internet so much!

"Dude! You are right. So unethical of me. I should not be so rough on the 'elite' allowing us to use Internet. I should mention the good side of the chaos! Well yes, we are allowed to have some fun, watch cat videos and send dick and boob pictures to each other! Heck thanks, how open handed you all are! After more than 20 years of the WWW being in our lives, the service of all Internet service providers is unprofessional, complex to deal with, expensive, while most online applications have been made for the convenience of the developer behind each application and not for the common end user. As long as we use it recreationally, dick pics are of an essence, until we attempt to use it professionally. In this circumstance Internet becomes super expensive, it does not work. As for the red tape has, it has no end, since this is no allowed, the other facility is not available, and the list goes…

It's surreal that more than two billion people use the internet almost every day, but in reality, we use less than 1% of what is actually uploaded on the worldwide websites.

Why whatever lies in the remaining 99% of online data is inaccessible to the rest of us?

Apart from the fact that it's easier to press the 'off' button for the 1% of the whole infrastructure when there is any attempt to leak out the real news, the 99% will remain intact for all necessary money making corrupt tactics, but most importantly controlling the masses and a potential coop and we have seen such examples year after year! So yes, Internet is there to save the world."

"Sir, Mr. superhuman", a man hollered from the far back of the room:
"The last comment for the 'off' button is against the Human Rights Act, globally accepted and applied even in the most deprived countries of our world. In other words, this declaration is our common moral language and I doubt that anyone from your alleged 'elite' would ever try to challenge that."

That is exactly what I mean, when I say reading off the script. In front of my eyes a manifestation of advanced levels of brainwashing, since the script was not read but has been memorized and repeated, when needed.

CHAPTER 21: INHUMAN RIGHTS IN DEFIANCE OF HUMAN RIGHTS

"How did you dare to create the term human rights, the biggest ever lie you call upon every crime you make against humanity, while fundamental aspects of the basis of a society are missing?

So it's your human right to live in prosperity and it's not a human right for the remaining 7 billion people to live with that same prosperity you do?

It's your human right to baptize yourself king and god and powerful, more physically and mentally developed and it's not our human right to have a chance to compete with you for this on an equal footing?

What are the human rights of all the people that your fake system ruled that they should now be in prison? Near to none.

When was the last time your fake system had a provision to assess its own part of the responsibility, that made those people commit a so-called crime against another human or the public common good? Almost never!

Why do you maintain a prison system that is there to make the majority of the so-called offenders worse than before they entered it?

Because there is a huge chain of profits, that support the sick economy you created from the minute one offends and then all the following steps down the line.

A key fact is that more than half of the offences committed worldwide have a direct relationship to drugs and weapons.

What have you achieved over the last century on the reduction of the available drugs and guns?

"Mr. Cornelius over the past 30 years we seize huge amounts of illegal substances almost monthly throughout the world. Our police, intelligence and army services have recorded big wins on the war on drugs. You are being unfair to a system trying its best against this organized type of crime", a man with some emotion said from the middle right of the room.

Another brainwashed key worker of the 'elite', that he cannot see his part of failure?

"I hear your comment, however, if we were able to freeze time at this very moment and develop a way to measure and compare the available resources for stopping drug trafficking over the cartels infrastructure, you will clearly see for yourself that your alleged war on drugs is unquestionably 100% unsuccessful, but at the same time it happens to be 100% profitable for all corrupt corporations. I will give you that, you do let us have a bit of fun sniffing cocaine and smoking marihuana until you put us in the nick. It's hilarious when at the same time you let the bigtime class A drug distributer have a dozen mansions, a few private jets and replacing their luxury yacht every couple of years. You criminalize the end user and use the big-time distributer to bring up or down entire governments. Its breakfast for the rich and war lords with your blessings.

As for the gun trade, creating demand for unjustified wars and defense upgrades for your puppet countries, it has been the most uninterrupted growing multibillion industry since we have recorded history. An evolution based on weapons led the human race to military breakthroughs.

In the 19th century you created the navy and army. In the 20th century you brought the air force coupled with nuclear capability. In the early 21st century we have the bio and cyber weapons with less clue of their capabilities and their level of destruction, while at the same time they are faster than all in delivery and effect. This latest technology comes to bring a change from the usual dull press conference script of your puppet press minister saying:

'we are going to war' which always meant in reality, *'we'*, thousands of dead; *'are'*, money billions; *'going'*, more of them dead; *'to'*, another country to acquire; *'war'*, proof of our failure.

Actually, there wouldn't even be that press conference, because you won't even let us know it's unleashed. This new technology makes it easy to make biological weapons on anyone's phone handset with the person next door becoming a nanotechnology technician, printing lethal DNA sequences that when deployed airborne or in a water stream, could cause a civilization to crash. That way you easily have many to blame for a directed outburst that could wipe out the human race for good. Mark my words, either deliberately or accidentally someone will do it and don't be surprised, if no one is left alive to take the blame."

Many of them looked down and that was a good sign or at least a pretentious moment of remorse. However, I wouldn't be surprised if many of the people in here thought of themselves as humanitarians and have felt offended by my tough demonstration. Either way, it's better that I can't read their minds, and I say that with very much self-control and responsibility!

CHAPTER 22: MEDIO-CRATIC MEDIA

"One would expect that the media would enhance togetherness, free us from our limitations of physical reality, but instead they are pulling us apart. Wasn't the main reason for the existence of the media, being the information medium, informing us of the problems and indicating potential solutions?
Why has this now completely shifted to broadcasting the news for entertainment with the primary aim to evoke specific emotions in the viewer, serving once more the 'attention economy'?
Tapping into our digital brain filters, the media is constantly feeding us with visual and sound stimulations, that most of the time lead us to an alternate reality.
Years ago, people got information from the newspaper, the next generation from television which invaded in our houses, leading us to nowadays where the Internet is now the trusted news source for most people with an unavoidably decreased time for fact checking.

"You look a man of his word, Cornelius", a man sitting comfortable on his chair said and he continued,
"You know for sure that most people in this room have got their news over the years through the stages

you described. The newspaper, television and now the online platforms. This is a healthy progression of media technology, resulting into faster communication of the headlines. A product of advancing evolution and I cannot figure how would you manage to turn this into a negative aspect of our society?"

"Well, Mr. comfortable on the chair, stay as you are and listen how!

Our attention, the attention of our partner, family, friend, and social circle has become the product, since it is not humanly possible to process all that information out there, fake or real, daily.

A news feed feels like entertainment for many of us, thus when we come across validated information, that most likely is the real news, we consider it boring and maybe untrue! The media determines who says 'it', when 'it' says it, what 'it' is they say, but most importantly determines who the end receiver is of that one-way form of information.

There you go once more, a tool of our 'evolved' society that apart from not doing what it's supposed to do, i.e. deliver the real news and watch over the powerful so they don't become corrupt, it's solely owned by the powerful! Jackpot for the 'elite', you got us on that one, as well.

Ask yourselves, what is the most important aspect of a successful bank robbery or escaping a bite from a dog chasing you? Creating diversion!

The powerful using the media for the sake of the

'elite', to create a diversion that keeps us occupied with petty entertaining news, by promoting mediocre products and most often promoting fear, meanwhile leaves aside the real social issues that we should really be thinking of.
There are so many different tactics, all used daily.
Think when you thought that the media were exaggerating a problem in order to gain attention. Then they released information gradually, forming an image of products or idiots they want you to pass for saints. Postponing big decisions, letting us take the news 'deep' in but slowly. Being overly kind, using the imperative form targeting our core feelings and in many cases our children. Keeping us uninformed without a proper level of education. Making us feel guilty for local as well as global uneasiness, that have already been orchestrated perfectly.
A complex relationship with every human being, the media has been exploited by the continuous propaganda and publicity forces, to shift our perception of reality in directions that suit the plans of mass control. Media tap upon each humans' desire to contextualize our experiences in regard to the others around us. We evolved into a culture where we watch what others do, so that we structure our next steps according to the preset norm that others also follow.

If this wasn't enough, there is constant development of the so called new, faster communication and mind control technologies that intended to help humanity, but instead all have one ultimate aim, mass control with the maximum effect, less effort and time.

The rapid change of the human race, its connection to something bigger, the connection of technology to biology and biology to electronics, is making the concerns we had of the negative effects of environmental DNA restructuring of humans, look like it never existed. We are all so addicted to technology, especially today's young people including kids, who will be the future adults. Beginning with hold able technology, switching into the wearable and moving fast to the inside the body technology, where instead of now queuing to get the latest gadget, our grown up kids in a few years will be queuing to get 'uploaded' and 'updated' with artificial intelligence technology, right through to their brain and the rest of their body's biological system.

We have been hacked of our working together abilities with swarm and deep learning artificial intelligence methods. In addition, our perceptual subconscious and to an extent our conscious is now extremely familiar with through preemptive programming, and ready to join the future synthetic humanoid army. All of which is already controlled through the artificial intelligence grid coupled with the virtual reality effect.

Media has done an excellent work pitching all that to the unsuspected young people as the better future world, presenting a reality where this type of humans can all be superhumans! If this isn't taking advantage of the new generation's naivety which even after all those fights for human independence, they would gladly trade it for dependence on the futuristic made for mass control corporations, what is?"

CHAPTER 23: NATURE'S LAST CALL

"You took the lead and we followed like sheep, to destroy apart from everything on it, the planet itself.
In comparison to the planet's existence and human life on it, it's a short period of time that it took you to discover oil and rely on that discovery for almost the entire economic growth and sustainability of our species on it, assuming its perpetuity. We have reached a state now that our current wellbeing is directly linked to how much oil we consume, resulting in a dependency that has become the vulnerability of our species. Even us nobodies know that the oil will eventually come to an end, sooner than that, this drainage of oil will cause problems to the Earth itself. But you clearly never cared about all of this, as long as your pockets were full of petrol money.
There are a vast number of reports that a significant decline of ice in the arctic will occur way before the end of the 21st century and it has already begun as I stand here before you. And what will happen with the carbon released from this melt down? Oh, nothing much!
We will just offset within the next 10 years all the carbon savings we were supposed to be generating for the next 50 years, ending up with us facing devastation on the planet on a scale that the best environ-

mental scientist cannot even imagine.
You think it's ridiculous to say that buying apples from another country and everyday shopping links to the global meltdown, but those very little acts of consumption link to a much bigger picture with visible signs of a collapsing ecosystem.
Greenhouse gasses are at their highest levels ever, the ice caps are melting fast, sea levels are rising. It's not a question anymore of if it's happening, but how quick it will change the way we live. What greatly saddens me is that as I am looking at all of you in here, you have made your 'exit plans', so that the impact of destroying the planet, will not affect you in the same way as all other humans. Either it be a bunker deep under the Earth's surface, an airplane fleet to refill in the air for years or a way to another planet, it is criminal.

With the little I know, I keep asking myself, what your plan was. If you ever had one, was it to use as much possible fossil fuel, so you fast track the melting of ice in order to have easier access to another new area of fossil fuel? How can you be as careless?
Your exploitation of the earth has caused the soil that we rely on for food and water, to reduce the nutritional value of most of the products by almost 40% at least over the last half of the 20th century. Imagine what we think we eat today. The quantities of most important metals underground are down by over 50% worldwide. We consume the last provisions of the Earth, knowing that for example water has no

substitutes and once we run out of it, we run out of life. Keep up the overconsumption of everything as we do and we will soon need 3 more planets like Earth to keep the existing numbers of human race going, something that is not an option, except if you know something, I don't!

Therefore, you are going to make us the only species that monitored and recorded each step of our own extinction, while we destroyed the visible nature in the name of 'invisible gods'. We all have been so accustomed to accept the changing climate of the Earth in a chaotic and destructive way, than to accept the prospect of changing the fundamental logic of capitalism based on growth and profit hunting."

An older man from the far back of the room got up and with a slow pace said:

"I personally have no bunker or anything of such in my name and will never have one. I appreciate that our planet's sustainability is facing tough times. However, this is another matter we are always looking into, as well as monitoring the environmental changes closely."

"And where did this 'monitoring' get you up until today?

Here, having given all the reasons of the world to a nobody superman telling you off big time. Do you think this is because I have nothing better to do or because I will never accept that none of your so-called advisors came to present alternative sources of energy?

And you ditched them! Especially knowing that the

fossils are running out, after you have blindly juiced the Earth way above its limits without having an estimate of unquestionably knowing when the planet is going to collapse.

I am sure they brought up geothermal, solar or kinetic plans to replace this raping of our planet. And I am sure that if I ask you where those plans are now, you have no clue. If I ask you what budget you have made available for such projects, you will not know. But I won't ask you what your army and new skyscrapers funding has been, because you will know, and I will lose my cool in here.

What about the different startups created by aspiring scientists that can harvest energy from seeds, plants and a myriad other way, including all the waste that can be further used to at least not be detrimental for the environment and the future of our species. Why are huge budgets not invested into those? Why is this not your top priority?"

CHAPTER 24: ACCOUNT-ABILITY OF THE SHEEP

"After all this time, don't tell me you don't expect me to do some self-criticism?
That I exclusively believe the fault of the current state of society is one sided and only blame the powerful. What about us common sheep?"

It was like hell broke loose. They began chattering like no tomorrow,

"It was about time,"
"He will turn it around and blame us again,"
"Right on spot,"
"I am sure he is messing with us now,"
"He kept it for the end,"
"That would be a break,"
"I don't have high hopes,"
"Now I need a drink,"
"I didn't see that coming."

At some point I had to stop them:

"That is enough people, I can hear you, you know, superman here, remember?
I just ask myself for a moment, when was the last time that I didn't support the greedy side of capitalism?
Well, I can't remember, because the answer is probably never.

Why do we common people have to choose sexy lingerie for our partner, when there is no way back from a failing relationship?
Why do we have to buy expensive handbags and high heels to make our better halves feel happy?
Why do we choose an expensive handset, that was produced in a country from a workforce consisted from women that live on rice and eventually will jump out the window to kill themselves one day?
And why then put this bloody handset in our fur coat, which was made after an animal trap was used to aid in its extinction?
Why go to online media to spill some misery on people, who most likely we don't even know and then funnily enough update our public profile with the hope that someone, somewhere gives a damn. Then after such a good timeline of actions, making capitalism even stronger, chill out, have a couple of cheap drinks or even better use any of the 'prohibited substances', heroin, cocaine or marihuana and keep wishing you had done most of the things in your life differently. Hey, at the same time you don't try to learn from the mistakes you made and continue making them again and again every day, allowing history to repeat itself in your own utopic disappointment. Keep up the good work, being the firefighter, doctor and teacher getting paid a fraction of the money you really deserve, that last only long enough for feeding the part of the capitalist engine you sustain. And yes, do all of these while you find happiness wearing blood diamonds, smoking the taxed 'killing you

slowly' cigarettes and watching the footballers and bankers making millions.

All of the above of course depending on the country you live in, because if natural selection got you in one of the poorer countries, then it is another story for you. For example, 10 countries at this time of human evolution harbor 80% of the poor and 70% of the illiterate of the world. In this case there are other plans for you. Human trafficking comes first, similarly as is done to animals. One or another form of slavery follows up next. And if you are lucky enough to survive both or either, get ready to be the perfect candidate for modern world exploitation. You see there is a plan for everyone, no one goes wasted, right?

The state of the planet today is our fault and not solely the fault of the capitalistic 'elite' of our society. It is we the common people, that have done nothing to prevent this outcome and if at this time of human evolution, we don't realize that we are all getting damper as every day passes, then that is the proof. A large percentage of humans including myself and everyone I know, are growing in a superficially comfortable environment without any challenge whatsoever and that is getting worse by the hour. Infertility in western countries is growing. We end up with a steady reduction of the educated, free minded people and overpopulate the planet with unchallenged and old people.

For the masses 'human development' has no meaning anymore. By restricting the ability of humans to think, express their opinion openly, be considered as important beings, it steadily compels them to feel small, unimportant, subsequently hindering human development on the whole.

We never asked ourselves, when are we going to stand up against our ruling empires and get our countries back?
Where are the peaceful demonstrations?
Where is the revolution in our own consciousness, dare to think differently and breaking the cubicle?
Why forget that our founded beloved nations have turned into empires and that we can restore our own national ideals without the need for military or any kind of arms. An intellectual revolution should happen by simply working together with aspirations for a better world.
We must bring back our humanity ideals to avoid having ten generations down the line looking back at us all and say, 'how did you all allow this to happen?' When they may be living in a fully controlling state, digitalized and without any access to blue sea, sky and wildlife in the forests. The future generations will never forgive us.

This is the final show down, we either fight peacefully with our human creativity and imagination and we take our birth right planet back in the next few years or sooner than we believe the level of destruction will be irreversible.

CHAPTER 25: A FAIR OPPORTUNITY IN A UTOPIC COLLECTIVE

Looking back over the centuries, you see a multi trillion charade theatrical production with capitalists, amateur capitalistic puppets, professional public sector highest officials, behind the scenes 'professionals' and a funding source (the 'elite'), creating an undeveloped planet with an overdeveloped history.
You kept concealing human history or made it unavailable for the most to know, clues that reveal our ability to understand Earth and its surroundings, 'the true furniture of the universe', believing that this is something you can also exploit for your own benefit.
You capitalized on the fact that humans are the only living organisms for whom 'I' and 'afraid of death' has an innate existential meaning. Fundamentally this created anxiety and coupling it with exogenously environmental stimulations, a degradation of the original DNA make up of our species leads us to a fast paced extinction.
Why do all of us 7 billion current 'tourists' on the planet and a large number of over 100 billion people who have lived on the planet previously, have to be the 'blood hosts' for the few to live comfortably?

Centuries of living in a complex capitalistic system with a disproportional rise to large inequality, pla-

cing at the forefront of this scandalous era, the poor free market fundamentalists. What these people are trying to do, is to convince us that the free market is universal and works well for all, whereas in fact the free market only works well for the rich and powerful. You say in between the lines, that if the rich get richer, we all benefit, the wealth will be available for all to get a feel.
Did you include the billions of people, who cannot drink water and have no food whatsoever, nor a house to sleep in at night?
You have supported throughout this time, the bullying approach that competition makes us better. Newsbreak, it doesn't! Because guess what, there is something else, it's called, cooperation and that does work better.

You had your chance over many centuries, to prove that this unequal distribution of wealth would achieve something for most humans, the planet and the future. Look at the planet today, the 21st century and you decide, whether your leadership was successful, aiding to the wellbeing of the most.

I can only assume by now, some of you in here will have felt a bit sad, not because you have just realized how much you have damaged this planet and all the species living on it, but because at some point you tried to do the right thing or have actually done it in one way or another. Guess what, it wasn't enough, and you know it!
So, don't even try telling me that 'I have repeatedly

given to charity to thousands of people and helped entire countries'.

You know better than me, that the day you had to answer the question, 'am I really making a difference here or not', you knew the answer was no. You knew that making a real difference would mean getting out of your comfort zone, out of the millionaire club, open the doors that you always had closed.

If you think you did something to save the life of one, two or several thousands of people, ask yourself, what about the remaining 7 billion people?

I know for sure, even just to show off, no one in this room is going to man up and admit out loud in front of every other 'colleague' in here, that you have lost the plot with everything, completely. I can still see it in the fake remorseful looks in your eyes, you still believe that you are some kind of the chosen ones. For the religious people in the form of higher spiritual leaders and for all the other simply privileged to be born on top. I hope for your own souls, that it won't be too late when you realize you are not neither of those. You are just the result of one of your father's lucky sperm cells, getting there first to fertilize the uterus of your mother, possibly the most excited sperm due to the alcohol your father consumed the night he was 'loving' your mother. That only is enough to make you just one of us and nothing more. All lucky enough to be born and get a chance to live on this planet, deserve a fair opportunity of living in a utopic collective, that has no hierarchy as we have experienced it. All are equal in a transcendent world that would connect all consciousness through fairness. So, I don't believe you are that idiotic, you would have guessed by now, the time has come to begin making some concrete changes towards our birthright.

CHAPTER 26: TAKE IT OR LEAVE IT

I am the 7 billion people! Somehow, I am their voice! I am them united, acting one day, at the same time, for one purpose, freedom! Enough of this quietness, we now choose to be free.

As opposed to what your ancestors did, you currently keep doing what you and your progenies are programmed to do. I will break this rule of yours and yes, I will give you options to choose from, more than one. Like it or not! Either you rectify 'it' (less than 4 years' work), either I will help the common people rectify 'it' (less than 2 years' work) or I shall rectify 'it' (less than a week's work!). Life as we know it, will change.

You might think, rectifying the wrongs you have done to the planet, would take decades to repair. You will see, it won't. Don't even think of telling me 'but how will we get this done, the time frame is too short' and all those lazy bum excuses. You go for it like you are all superman.

Option one will be the best option for all of you, getting one chance to correct all wrong doings.

This is how it will go. All banks, bankers and associated money 'elite' handlers will give back all the money they have stolen over the last century, to all the governments and common people with interest, say only 30%. In simpler terms, all the money stolen with inflation, unfair interest values, capital bubble bursts, trade markets, tax evasion, paper money cutting and selling bankrupt companies, shall I continue, or do you get the point?

The room went on fire, some got up, others, fell off their chairs and chattering prevailed.
"Oh, that is preposterous,"
"He doesn't mean me,"
"Everything I have is in my wife's name,"
"I can sell everything on bitcoin,"
"Is he having a laugh, 30% interest?"
"He is messing with us,"
"I have to call my solicitor,"
"Relax people, there are two more options!"

"Quiet everyone, the real monologue begins now,"

I had to shout which each time meant a tremor in the room that made them settle down.

"To settle those debts to humanity, would take, say 6 months, max! Then, once this 'equalization payback' is completed, all of you 'chosen ones' will pay back to the states you live in the money your ancestors stolen, say in the form of tax. Simply put, all humans will pay x tax and you and 50 generations down the line will have to pay x times 3, monthly! That way, maybe at some point your unborn children and grandchildren will pay back the majority of the debt for you and your ancestors criminal ripping off the humanity. This might minorly equalize the centuries of stolen money and life of billions of people slaved."

The room remind me the funeral I went for my boss's father, and who can tell me now that I bought that suit for only one funeral.

"Then you will generate one currency worldwide! So, no more trading and selling currencies. Guess what, I leave it to you to name it!
You will completely stop any tax avoidance and there will be no more tax heavens!
New laws in place that you will pass in week one, will clearly indicate that it will be life imprisonment for tax avoidance without the possibility of parole. That key move will make any remaining rich crooks land back down to Earth for good.
You will set a proper living wage for all, worldwide. The minimum hourly salary will be 200% up from what it is today in every country of the world and for any kind of job. This will also be the salary that all high-end bankers, solicitors, actors, footballers, politicians, and CEOs will be getting for as long as humanity exists. At the same time all medical staff, public servants and people working on the front line for new sustainable development goals, will be getting paid the top available salaries, i.e., what all of the above are earning today!
Human rights will be applied for all humans alive and be enforced everywhere, regardless. No one would be allowed to die from a mosquito bite, starvation, water deprivation or have no house to live in.
You will stop the monopoly of the press and you

will make private companies that are owned by the people of the local town without major shareholders. No single person will ever again owe 51% of a single company.

All these initial steps have to do with giving the power back to the common people, the space and time to come together. This could be the equality needed for co-operation for one main purpose apart from our survival, our species gradual and productive development.

All private banks will not be allowed to earn money from money anymore. Which means, you give them time to close down, we don't need them. Only regulated state banks will do the lending and would be able to earn money from money, so that profits can go back to the citizens and their states. Interest on lending would be justified in a manner that this will be the income of the bank to pay its employees, period. We don't need rich banks anymore, we need banks with money used to serve a purpose, not to serve them. You will make all private drug companies, public and they will prescribe legal drugs, free of charge. As for the illegal drugs, you will make the drug barons sell their 'products' for productive sustainability and medical purposes and if they don't, shut them off within a month. You can and you know how, period.

There will be no royals anywhere ever again. You want to call yourself a royal, suit yourself. You open a museum following the company formation outlined above and give a ticket to anyone wanting to come and see how your ancestors and you were ripping humanity off over the centuries. No government funds will ever be spent on royalty, no so-called royal will own anything but what they earn from their morning jobs.

You will cease all country to country challenges for border pushing and power sprees. Borders of all countries are as set today, period. No more military budgets of any kind, no more production of weapons of any kind. The existing weapons will be within a few decades, antiques, to simply remind you how much you had lost your way throughout the previous centuries. No more budgets for space programs of any sort. You will keep the existing space technology and will maintain it, ready to be picked up again once you have secured and brought planet Earth and all the people living on it back to where it should have been. No more budgets for cloud technologies. Internet and all associated technology coming with it, will be used for communication purposes and aiding achieving the targets described hereafter. Existing and new budgets will be spent on two main fronts. The first and most important will be for sustainability development goals, including food, housing and public health without any negative emissions for the environment whatsoever. The second would be on medical research, solving everything that kills humans. In addition, all public transportation will be nearly free for all. All private sea and air transportation will pass from private to public control. A fee for travelling will be paid by all civilians in the form of tax, based on the expenses related to paying the employees, maintenance and advancing of the equipment used.

Prisons will cease to exist in the current form. From now on, they will all be local government production factories, which will have all the necessary provisions to help inmates get back on their feet and realize this one chance in a lifetime. You will teach them what's right from wrong, provide them with all necessary support and for the remaining time of their 'sentence' based on their skills and abilities will be working for the production factory. If some are 'uncurable', they will stay in these 'production factories' forever. No more death sentences.

And here we are, I have some goodies for all of you in here as well as your 'elite' buddies. None of you that you are now at the top of the food chain, will be prosecuted for your crimes against humanity, as long as you spend all your excess money to help all humanity get back on its feet. You will make sure you channel all resources to end the poverty you created for centuries. You will have 4 calendar years until your first and only hearing and if you adjust to this new pragmatic society, your crimes against society will be waived forever!

Once more, the room felt like I created a tremor, but it wasn't me this time,

"What did he mean by that?"
"I will have to ask for an extension,"
"Can we combine years as per family?"
"Who would be charring the hearing?"

"The 4 years start counting from today?"
"What does he mean by common people?"

"Next time this rampage of chattering goes on, I will have to..." and everyone did shut it for good this time,

"You have 4 years to shift from the kind of people addicted to this short-term consumption fix and greediness, to the people we depend on the most for changing the way the world works for an alternative vision that respects the planet's hospitality to our species.
Once you begin achieving these targets, I bet you will be surprised by the human nature found within you that you suppressed so much for centuries. We are all going to be slowly seeing the participation in the general elections increase, crime will begin dropping, depression as well as the so-called terrorism will become history and the real culture of each country will flourish again.

With all this said, you do understand that this is one chance I will give you to become the saviors of the planet and human civilization, while my existence will be kept secret. In other words, all the positive things for the real greater good will feed back and be accounted to you. This is one in a lifetime chance. I will be monitoring everything you will be doing from the shadows and be sure, if I pick up a deviation from those plans or an opportunistic move that benefits the few, I will intervene without giving you a second chance, be sure of it.

Guess what I left for last?"

I could see now in their faces the definition of panic,

"Relax people, it's the easiest of all.
You get another aspect of this new era to name it whatever you want, this new economic system! Ha-ha-ha," realizing I was the only one laughing in the whole room. I could suspect, why they didn't find that funny at all!

"The second option I am about to give you is somewhat trickier, while I again will keep my identity secret and simply make your system look vulnerable.
I will punch holes in your system and even the most unsuspecting human being on the planet will believe they have an opportunity to benefit from it. I can get from one side of the planet to the other in seconds and most importantly without anyone seeing me doing it, while at the same time I can organize all the humans in every country against you all and your capitalistic regimes.

I have several ways of doing it but for the sake of it, I will only share a few with you. Your system is strong but with many loopholes that would allow me to enter and dismantle it from the inside.
I can begin convincing people to simply stop using the below average quality tools, services and products you offer them. What would happen if the majority of people in one of the supposedly developed countries, stopped using public transport, shopping at the malls and supermarkets, using their credit

cards and all processes for lending from banks was frozen? You know very well, if they did it gradually, you might be able to adjust and cope for some time, but in the long term, your system would collapse. What if this is a coordinated effort and a very large number of people made this move all in the same day? Your system would go down like a stone in the sea.

Think for a second, what if I get everyone to do what is so easy to do. Call in sick all on the same day or even the same week! The teacher at school, the doctor at the hospital, the firefighter at the disaster, the police officer on the street, the soldier at the ludicrous country invasion and the list goes on. Your corrupt system can be brought down so easily. With a little bit of organization, humans can do most of those, by themselves, without me in the picture. But it will really depend on how much time I want to spend on it all and how much effort I am willing to make. I have superpowers and you have seen a fraction of them, don't forget that.

Another approach I might take is that I could easily take out your 'cloud' and all associated hard copies of who owes what to whom. Done and dusted in a few hours. No one in this world will be able to track or have any kind of proof of a previous transaction. Once the word is out, people will go out on the streets celebrating. As you see, I could keep handing the common people big wins. Simple fun stuff for me, as they go out in your main cities and you deploy the riot police and army, I will disable all of your key communications, while I will leave the people's communications as they are! Like that, I will be giving the impression to the people that they are winning, and more will keep coming out on the streets in more countries.

The fun for me could never end with this second choice. Another thing I can do would be opening a few thousand supermarket stores around the world that do deliver at home! Don't tell me that you don't secretly laugh a bit with that now! Well, yes you do. It sounds lame I know. But what if I tell you that you will pay for it! Still laughing? Hm, let's see. I rip off some of your banks. I doubt you will go out to say, superman did it. Here is where I laugh. I will then go to all the small food producers around the world in each country and pay them with your money, double what you give them now to work like slaves for your giant supermarket corporations. I will then take those products that cover everything one needs to live on and provide them to my supermarkets for free, for all! Like a real charity, you know like the ones you pretend you have. Just think about it, how long will your supermarket giants keep their doors open for, if sales drop, to 70% in the first month, to 50% in the second month and below 20% thereafter? Because I still suspect there would be some jackasses amongst the common people that would prefer to come and pay to buy your deadly products.

I can do the same for everything you provide as a service to the poor people of Earth at the moment.

A fair prediction would be that it will take way less than a year to bring your regimes down all around the world and another year for the people to take the power back into their own hands on their own terms this time, something that took you decades to orchestrate. Would you like to take your chances, be my guest...?

And there you go now, I have your uninterrupted full attention! Let me pleasantly give you my third and fastest to be enforced option.

I will go public, introduce myself exactly as I did to you. I will demonstrate my powers to all. Then I will set a clear question to the citizens of this planet.
Do they want me to take over the planet, spread the wealth to all and make you pay for your crimes against humanity?
We let the 7 billion decide and we will have no choice but to act upon it."

The room was now literally a cemetery. There was not a single sound in there. You see, even after all that 'lecturing' none of them want the common people climbing the ladder.

"Oh, relax people! If I were an egomaniac like you have been throughout your life, I would have taken option three without even asking you.
And imagine if I had told you the even better idea that crossed my mind a few days ago, but I would leave that to your imagination...
I hope now you can picture the different options on the table and how clear they are. Now, take this as if you were dreaming all that time, living on your own utopic planet and suddenly someone woke you up

and the first face you saw, was mine, smiling at you! It could have been worse, don't you think?

I know it won't be that easy from now on, since you cannot save the whole world in one day, because you are not me, but if you begin saving the world as individual people, you will end by saving the world much faster than you could have ever imagined."

A slightly less than 5-hour 'lecture' that I wanted to have the opportunity to give once in my lifetime with this audience in particular. I felt virtuous and I flew out of the room before they realized how and where from. I flew up in the blue sky above the entire city and soon I could see the whole country. I hovered and looked down one more time. I wasn't sure, what was I hoping they would do.

CHAPTER 27: A DREAM COMES TRUE

Within minutes I was back home, landing inconspicuously a bit further down the road and walked in my flat. I sat on the couch and I just couldn't believe what I have just done. I was ecstatic. Although I haven't thought much what the timeframe of would be for waiting to see what they would do, I had to take a break from all of it. I closed my eyes for a rest.

I woke up at some point late in the evening. I clearly needed that sleep, even I fi was superman!
My phone had several missed calls.
The general peripheral noise from the inside of my flat and surrounding area had increased.
There was something vibrant all over the place and I couldn't figure what. I got up and looked outside the window.
I could see people walking in and out of the ad hoc area.
What the heck was going on?

I went back to my phone to check the missed calls. I had several from my wife, a couple from my mother, Kostas called once and even my manager from work had left a voicemail. Either I was exposed, or they missed me...

Still, I wasn't buying it. I opened the TV and sat again on the couch.
What was different this time was that the news anchor was standing on the side of the screen instead of being sat looking bored. I turned up the volume of the TV and there it was in front of all humanity. The representatives of the 'elite', lined up one after another coming up to the stand making some really bold statements:

"Today's summit was like no other,"
"After extensive discussions we decided to hear for good the voice of mother Earth, no more fossil fuels,"
"Tax money will go back to the people,"
"We don't need private banks,"
"Unjustified asset repositions will be returned back to all people,"
"The time has come to reward public servants, medical staff and front-line workers,"
"We will prioritize support for new and old small businesses,"

They kept going on and on, even mentioning new positive plans that I hadn't suggested.
I had given them a chance that none of us would ever get in a lifetime.
I made a wish that humanity would choose the correct option and it did, so that in the future we would all have another good bedtime story to tell from our perspective! That was it, job done for me.

My next biggest thought was about the coming weekend. My wife wanted to have lots of sex, how can I forget. One thing just occurred to me, do you think I will have superkids with Ursula?

Printed in Great Britain
by Amazon